MW01274233

This Here's
a Merica

Books by LOUIS DANIEL BRODSKY

Poetry

Five Facets of Myself   (1967)* (1995)
The Easy Philosopher   (1967)* (1995)
"A Hard Coming of It" and Other Poems   (1967)* (1995)
The Foul Rag-and-Bone Shop   (1967)* (1969)* (1995)
Points in Time   (1971)* (1995) (1996)
Taking the Back Road Home   (1972)* (1997)
Trip to Tipton and Other Compulsions   (1973)* (1997)
"The Talking Machine" and Other Poems   (1974)* (1997)
Tiffany Shade   (1974)* (1997)
Trilogy: A Birth Cycle   (1974) (1998)
Cold Companionable Streams   (1975)* (1999)
Monday's Child   (1975) (1998)
Preparing for Incarnations   (1975)* (1976) (1999) (1999 exp.)
The Kingdom of Gewgaw   (1976)
Point of Americas II   (1976) (1998)
La Preciosa   (1977)
Stranded in the Land of Transients   (1978)
The Uncelebrated Ceremony of Pants Factory Fatso   (1978)
Birds in Passage   (1980)
Résumé of a Scrapegoat   (1980)
Mississippi Vistas: Volume One of *A Mississippi Trilogy*   (1983) (1990)
You Can't Go Back, Exactly   (1988) (1988) (1989)
The Thorough Earth   (1989)
Four and Twenty Blackbirds Soaring   (1989)
Falling from Heaven: Holocaust Poems of a Jew and a Gentile
    (with William Heyen)   (1991)
Forever, for Now: Poems for a Later Love   (1991)
Mistress Mississippi: Volume Three of *A Mississippi Trilogy*   (1992)
A Gleam in the Eye: Poems for a First Baby   (1992)
Gestapo Crows: Holocaust Poems   (1992)
The Capital Café: Poems of Redneck, U.S.A.   (1993)
Disappearing in Mississippi Latitudes: Volume Two of *A Mississippi
    Trilogy*   (1994)
A Mississippi Trilogy: A Poetic Saga of the South   (1995)*
Paper-Whites for Lady Jane: Poems of a Midlife Love Affair   (1995)
The Complete Poems of Louis Daniel Brodsky: Volume One, 1963–1967
    (edited by Sheri L. Vandermolen)   (1996)

Three Early Books of Poems by Louis Daniel Brodsky, 1967–1969: *The Easy Philosopher*, *"A Hard Coming of It" and Other Poems*, and *The Foul Rag-and-Bone Shop (edited by Sheri L. Vandermolen)* (1997)

The Eleventh Lost Tribe: Poems of the Holocaust   (1998)

Toward the Torah, Soaring: Poems of the Renascence of Faith   (1998)

Bibliography (Coedited with Robert Hamblin)

Selections from the William Faulkner Collection of Louis Daniel Brodsky: A Descriptive Catalogue   (1979)

Faulkner: A Comprehensive Guide to the Brodsky Collection
    Volume I: The Bibliography   (1982)
    Volume II: The Letters   (1984)
    Volume III: *The De Gaulle Story*   (1984)
    Volume IV: *Battle Cry*   (1985)
    Volume V: Manuscripts and Documents   (1989)

Country Lawyer and Other Stories for the Screen by William Faulkner   (1987)

Stallion Road: A Screenplay by William Faulkner   (1989)

Biography

William Faulkner, Life Glimpses   (1990)

Fiction

The Adventures of the Night Riders, Better Known as the Terrible Trio *(with Richard Milsten)*   (1961)[*]

Between Grief and Nothing   (1964)[*]

Between the Heron and the Wren   (1965)[*]

Dink Phlager's Alligator *(novella)*   (1966)[*]

The Drift of Things   (1966)[*]

Vineyard's Toys   (1967)[*]

The Bindlestiffs   (1968)[*]

Yellow Bricks   (1999)

Catchin' the Drift o' the Draft   (1999)

This Here's a Merica   (1999)

[*] *Unpublished*

This Here's
a Merica

Short fictions
by

L.D. Brodsky

TIME BEING BOOKS
POETRY IN SIGHT AND SOUND
St. Louis, Missouri

Time Being Books®
10411 Clayton Road
St. Louis, Missouri 63131

Time Being Books® is an imprint of Time Being Press®
St. Louis, Missouri

Time Being Press® is a 501(c)(3) not-for-profit corporation.

Time Being Books® volumes are printed on acid-free paper, and binding materials are chosen for strength and durability.

The characters and events portrayed in these stories are fictitious. Any similarities to real persons, living or dead, is purely coincidental and not intended by the author.

ISBN 1-56809-056-0 (Paperback)

Library of Congress Cataloging-in-Publication Data:

Brodsky, Louis Daniel.
    This here's "A merica" : short fictions / by L.D. Brodsky. — 1st ed.
      p.   cm.
    ISBN 1-56809-056-0 (pbk. : alk. paper)
    1. United States—Social life and customs—20th century Fiction.
  I. Title. II. Title: This here's America.
PS3552.R623T48   1999
813'.54—dc21   99-25320
                                              CIP

Book design and typesetting by Sheri L. Vandermolen
Manufactured in the United States of America

First Edition, first printing (1999)

Acknowledgments

For aiding and abetting me in this volume of an ongoing series of short fictions, I express my gratitude to the editorial staff at Time Being Books: former Editor in Chief, Jerry Call, his successor, Sheri Vandermolen, and the new Managing Editor, Jenny Agnew.

Each has worked toward the same goal, all the while making distinct contributions. Jerry Call is responsible for initially suggesting the possibility that I, a poet by profession, might indulge myself in writing various short fictions, which, to my great pleasure, I have done. Sheri Vandermolen has given to these fictions a clarity and continuity they would not otherwise have had. And Jenny Agnew has worked side by side with me, skillfully executing final revisions.

For Jerry Call,
my editor.

It just don't get no better.

Contents

A Tribute to the Living Dead *17*

A Hell of a Way to Make a Living *18*

The Market at a Glance *19*

Heaven's Gate Redux *21*

Fubar's *22*

Dropping Out: The Ultimate Therapy *27*

Junk-Mailed to Death *29*

Abiogenesis *31*

Half-Lives of Postmen, Poets, and Giant Talking Clams *33*

Upstaged *34*

Trapped at the Gasworks *39*

Space Traveler *41*

Keeping an Eye on Things *43*

"Making Chicken Salad Out of Chicken Shit": A Foreword by
  A. Colonel Lingus, to *So You'd Like to Try Your Hand at
  Writing for a Living*, by Executive Sous-Chef Hosea "Butch"
  Butcher of Lyons, Georgia *45*

Iced Ages *47*

Homo oneiricus *51*

Veteran Doorman *52*

Roswell *53*

Prince Metaphor, Archenemy of I-Am-Me *54*

In Effigy *57*

Q.T.'s in a Pinch *58*

A Personal Story *65*

Eat-Off Artist *67*

Patriarch of the Breakfast Table   *69*

Mr. No Longer   *72*

Brother Onan Takes Away the Sins of the World   *73*

Stupor Bowl Tailgate Key Party   *75*

Is What He Isn't, Ain't What He Was   *79*

Pogo Sticks   *81*

Bone Mot   *82*

A Surefire Shot at Heaven   *84*

Dream State o' the Onion   *86*

There Was an Old Man   *92*

Stabbed in the Back   *94*

Preowned-Vehicle Account Executive, Late Again   *95*

Lottie Savage, Colored   *96*

In the Brain-Terrain of the Walking Dead   *98*

Karla Mae   *100*

Settling for Unleavened Bread on the Road Out of Egypt   *104*

Dennis the Doorman   *106*

The Toad   *107*

Mr. Late-Nite TV   *109*

This Here's
a Merica

A Tribute to the Living Dead

It's Memorial Day, and no one's working today but facto-
tums, flunkies, and grunts, stiffs stuck in essential occupations
— waitresses, busers, and short-order cooks for seven-day-a-
week grab-it-and-runs, nurses and orderlies in hospitals and
hospices, hotel clerks and bellboys, transportation personnel,
athletes paid to entertain on TV, and, naturally (of course! oh,
well!), that pariah-tribe of absurdly obsessed makers — societal
misfits driven to build Great Walls of China, Lighthouses of
Alexandria, and pyramids of Giza single-mindedly, in an hour
or lifetime — and artists and inventors incapable of pulling
the plug, disengaging power from the psyche's grid, setting the
trip mechanism in case a Loch Ness monster breaks loose from
its cage at the far end of the brain's laboratory, where ten mad
scientists labor incessantly to discover a cure for dreaming.

No one's working, this Monday, no one but those creative
refugees and deportees, displaced waifs, who should be stay-
ing in bed, relaxing in indolence, for one morning at least,
enjoying a brief cessation of stress before resuming their Sisy-
phean tasks of beginning all over from scratch, on their backs,
each dawn, frescoing all of Creation on the ceiling of their
hearts' Sistine Chapels . . . no one, possibly, but me, CEO of the
Congress of Bottle and Window Washers, sacrificial goat of the
eleventh lost tribe, hand-carved cigar-store Native American
paleface on the bottom of the cosmic scrotum pole, overlook-
ing the twenty-third Valley of Psalm Springs, an intoxicated
pantaloon with a W.C. Fields start, an Oliver Hardy whimper,
a Charlie Chaplin all-day pratfall on a banana peel.

Yes, I'm the dumb bastard working his ass off, this Memo-
rial Day. It's the only way I can justify my stay. After all, who
else would shovel elephant shit from the circus's main ring,
ashes and bones from Topf ovens at Auschwitz, images and
symbols out of his imagination's sewers for Kapo's wages?
Who else but a dead poet?

A Hell of a Way to Make a Living

Recently, they've caught him in the act: perjuring him-
self black and blue in a high-profile televised trial, in which
he's accused of slicing his ex-wife and her Mezzaluna squeeze
on the doorsteps of her Brentwood digs; mixing fertilizer
with subversive diatribes to blow up Uncle Sam in Oklahoma
City; biting off a chunk of his opponent's ear in a glitzy Vegas
boxing match; trying to sell, through a Lithuanian cartel, tac-
tical nuclear missiles left over from the Cold War. They've
caught him cross-dressing as well, inventing "her" innocence
in the face of a court-martial for fraternizing and sodomizing
in the cockpit of "her" B-52, and, in a fit of misplaced passion,
cutting off "her" cheating husband's penis, as he dreamed his
doggy dreams, and throwing it in a nearby field to rot in Hell.

Ah, but what a clever devil he is, almost always dissolving
into the woodwork at the eleventh hour, getting a timely re-
prieve, reversal of cursed fate, the court's mercy, fading into
obscurity overnight, into the proverbial sunset over Malibu
or Fire Island.

He's a quick-change artist, carny barker, mojo/voodoo
necromancer, dark artificer, sleight-of-hand flimflam man,
master of ceremonial deceits, guru to buggers and thieves,
elusive advisor to tyrants, pirates, and the clergy, archfiend
of the nether world, protean demon, archetypal pretender
to the throne on High.

He's never been a fuddy-duddy, shrinking violet; indeed,
his brazenness is legendary. Today, he's touring Hong Kong,
as a nine-hundred-pound Beijing gorilla named Hung Dung,
who'll rule by the divine right of kings and reinstall all human
wrongs.

The Market at a Glance

Dear Lord, when will they learn, those pseudosavvy investors from America's hinterlands, those giddy new kids on Main Street's block, caught dead to rights, in broad daylight, with their fingers in the cookie jar, small-town prestidigitators tickled pink as pregnant pigs' tits, that vision isn't a Sphinx's riddle that serendipity, kismet, hubris, and miracles can answer with a stroke of their magic wands and that it isn't blind luck, fate, ESP, New Age hocus-pocus, divining-rod shamanism blessed by the Pope, lightning striking twice, five days a week, at the New York Stock Exchange, or tying a perfect double Windsor in the dark?

Oh, no! What those dumb bastards haven't yet figured out is that good fortune hedges its bets every chance it gets. It's all a vast grapevine the privileged use to communicate their insider information. Believe me, whether it gets consummated in a steamy Holmby Hills hot tub, Salt Lake City's Mormon Tabernacle Choir dressing rooms, a South Beach Miami gay juice-bar, Cape Cod's opulent WASPish compounds, or Manhattan's Jewish retro-ghettos, Wall Street listens when Buffet whispers, shits when Gates pinches a loaf, masturbates when Greenspan spanks the interest-rate monkey.

But what neither those good ol' boys in the boonies nor those descended-of-rubes New York analysts, money managers, estate planners have yet internalized, owned up to, in truth, are those two fundamental Newtonian laws of gravity: 1.) what goes up must plummet; 2.) at the core of every apple that drops on your head is a worm of some ilk, waiting to pulverize your earnings and spit out enough silk to cocoon your paralyzed carcass when you learn your mutual fund or diversified portfolio has been decimated, in one fell crash, by an unanticipated computer virus, "rogue trader," or surprise nuclear strike by the illegitimate stepson of Saddam

Hussein's concubine, taking revenge on the world for his syphilitic condition.

What else can I say, dear Lord? To be honest with you, I'm not a model citizen myself. I must confess, just yesterday, I phoned my broker, Moe Steinsaltz, and had him sell off all my shares of Boeing, Caterpillar, Motorola, and Coke, roll over my profits into Intel, Microsoft, Oracle, Cisco, and Dell. I mean, a friend of my ex-wife's former marriage counselor and my dentist's mistress, whom I've been seeing on the sly, both got wind that the NASDAQ was in for a 40 percent rise in the next five months. And who am I to miss out on a sure thing? Even Moe got excited, passed my tip along to all his clients.

Lord, not meaning to be presumptuous, but . . . You might want to get in on a good thing too, for a change.

Heaven's Gate Redux

He uses the weekends not to recuperate (he rarely sleeps more than three hours a night) but to catch down on finished business, loosen tied ends, decompose letters to potential and forgotten friends who never existed nor ever will, no matter how eloquent or affectionate, Delphic or Scriptural or Mapplethorpean he might wax on his sub-atomic, gracile-australopithecine electroencephalorosetta-encryptopornetoscope, which he never has to worry about booting up (he's not learned the first thing about cyberspeak except to hire jinns and goblins and dybbuks to do his bidding night and day), since he never shuts it off, instead lets its dish run away with the fork in the road in the hope that just once he might locate a kindred spirit in deep space, communicate with it, if not face to face, on a reasonably personal basis, strike an alliance with a higher life form, and justify dying, before someone on Earth identifies him, tongue-ties him down to Lilliput's ground zero, and insists he demonstrate the latest techniques in training zombies and vampires for societal survival, teaching them to convert toxic waste into snake oil, human feces into finger food, urine into Dom Perignon, and to pass a Breathalyzer test while pissing on the queen's castle from the tightrope they cross on Shriners' motorcycles.

Oh, if only he could grab the tail of the Hale-Bopp comet, fly through the universe like a hallucinogenic goose, he might justify dying as a corporate write-off, donate his remains to the Aliens Hall of Fame, and disappear for an endless weekend in Club Dead, where he might catch up on unfinished business, tie loose ends, compose letters to old friends, associates, alter his urges for altar boys, and rub shoulders with the rich, famous, and moonstruck.

Fubar's

If there was one, I swear there was twenty-five of 'em, systemally spaced out around the place like Eastern eggs hidin' in a junkyard, inconspiculous enough to flummox a eight-year-old, hidden axledently on purpose, boxed in under the ducks, around the pillars, all along behine the bar — them damn TVs, that is — so as to please 'n not obnox the payin' customers, them come in to eat the grub and them like me, come to down some suds, get down on my depressed selfs, wash my troubles out to sea, or, as they say about the redface Chief Lipton, who done drunk too much tea, drown in my teapee, seein' stars, countin' buffalo-sheeps leapin' over pressalpisses, which is precisely what I was fixin' to do after my eighth or ninth brew yesterday afternoon, 'cause to keep all that competin' sound from drum-beatin' my brains like they was tom-toms settin' up a war-dance beat just before they honed in on Custard's last scalp, a guy's gotta do somethin', 'specially since all I intended to do anyways was catch a few hours o' football at Fubar's, the sportin' bar over to Marconi 'n Flad, where I go to disappear off the faces o' the map every onced in the eyes o' March or so (even if it *is* the end o' September), just to allude the missus long enough to get my bearin's in a man's whirl again . . . this joint servin' up a mean burger-'n-chili combo, a extra-mean homegrown meatloaf plate with authentical, down-cuntry, slurpin'-thick gravy, Texass toast, 'n mashed garlic spuds, all o' which I treated myselfs to, despite my diet, before I even got to the serious beeswax at hand, which was to watch the Pittsburghs rout shit outten the Ten o' Seas Oilers, assumin', that is, a guy can keep sane for them twenty-five TVs all blarin' to onced, like five Mazy's Day parades all interweavin' on a Big Ten halftime gritiron, doin' them stupid maneuvers with tubals 'n tromboners bobbin' like elephump trunks runnin' under the circus tent on their grand entrance, like they was — each member o' Alexandria's On-the-Ragtime Band — a piece o' glass or a colored bead in a collide-o-scope gone apeshit.

I swear on a stack o' Gideon King Jimmys that if there's twenty-five TVs in Fubar's, there's a hunnerd 'n twenty-five o' them suckers, 'cause management (and that's another mystery) can't seem to get all twenty-five on the same channels — oh, no! No way! That'd be too damn easy 'n way too sane. They had five channels goin' to onced, at least four different games blarin' 'n slo-moin' 'n freeze-framin' 'n instant-replayin' 'n commentatin' with talkin' faces 'n squiggly lines — the whole nine yards, which don't really get you a first down when you're tryin' to concentrade on two teams 'stead o' eight, brawlin' 'n wranglin' to beat shit outten each other.

Truth is, when they got that much goin' to onced, a guy gets the dizzies even before the suds takes over, which, in my federal case, means not 'til I done crossed the Innernational Dated Line somewhere in the six-to-eight-brewsky Moluccas range, reached that Bud Light point o' no returns, where lizards 'n frogs 'n toads 'n things are unflatin' their dewflaps 'n pouches like crazy, stickin' their tongues out to lick up a unsuspectible inseck clean outten existence — fastest tongues in the west, 'cept for mine, that is, when I'm in unexceptionably very rare form, like on Friday nights with the missus — a kind o' sacrifacial right with me, a celebation on finishin' another week at the car plant, you know, like the Mayans o' ancient Mexico 'n the Peruvians o' Aztecia used to do, or, for that matter, like them Bible guys 'n Roamans, sacrifacin' theirselfs to vestibule virgins, so's to reprove their manhoods, reprove their viral desire for increasin' the tribes.

Anyways, as I was sayin', I'm tryin' like hell to concentrade on my game, but between them nonstop breaks to advertise brew (which don't fail to work a subriminable effect on me, makin' me chug faster, reorder more quicker), advertise Suburbarus 'n Izoozoo Jap Troopers 'n all manner o' useless products for baby bloomers, Generation XYZers, advertise stuff for effeminate hygenie 'n yeast inflections, machines

to take weight off your abs, butts, tits, love handlers, 'n cellular-
riddled legs, advertise debilatories, ginseng knives, Exlax-
atives. . . . Jeezus! Enough shit to make a man almost forget
his mission: just tryin' to watch one game, just *one*.

Of a suddlenly, I slump down in my seat 'n stare up. All I can
say is "Not to be not believed!" I mean, I see a caveful o' stalag-
tights all danglin' 'n hoverin' 'n shudderin' above me, flutterin'
in the crostdrafts rushin' helter 'n skelter from a dozen air-
conditionin' ducks, them stalag-tights becomin', on closer
perusal, unflatable balloons in the shapes o' lizards 'n frogs,
brew mugs, brew bottles, brew volleyballs, brew spaceships,
more frogs, and then I notice the place's got as many neon
signs as it do TV screens. Jeezus! There must be at least sixty-
nine neons, all lip-sinkin' each other, screamin' out in hot
pinks 'n blues 'n green neons — neon penguins, neon frogs,
neon lizards, neon spaceships, neon canoes, more frogs 'n
lizards, all blinkin' out "Budweiser, Budweiser, Budweiser."

Just then, one o' them harems o' high-school dropouts
(they could be Aztecias nor Mayans nor Peruvian-Mexicans)
they deploy here at Fubar's sidles up to me, me at least
twiced her age, eight times her extra-peteat size, here in
them Hooters-type, snatch-high, short-short shorts, wantin'
to know do I need somethin' else, eyein' me with one o'
them ponpond, come-whither stares that the boths of us
knows is just all part o' the act, the Atom-Eve-Snake act from
way back, where all parties concerned knows they got a
oblongation to further the "increase o' the tribe" bit for
old-time's snake, the way-of-all-flesh beeswax. So she rubs
up her very bare thigh against my hairy bicep, and I feel my
unit start to come alive, begin to quiver, make its presence
felt 'n known, if you catch the rub o' my grubworm, show
some interest in the outside whirls; I mean, what does it
know from eighteen-year-old nor the Man's Act nor sodomy
in Gomorrah, if you catch the drift o' my draft Bud? So I say
that come to think on it, there just could be somethin' she
might do for me.

"That's what we're here for, hon, to serve and protect,"
she says with a leer that's supposed to suggest she's a regu-
lar watcher o' *NYDT Blues* or some such cop drama on weekly
TV that shows hookers 'n homos panderin' in broad's day-
light, TV that, 'cept for Sunday afternoon 'n Monday 'n Thurs-
day nights 'n Saturday all day, I don't indulge, you might
say, 'less you include Friday-night Budweiser boxin' from
Lost Vagrants. And I'm thinkin', how's she gonna protect me?
From myselfs, maybe, who, deep in my secret self, wants to
repeat one o' them Inca fertilizin' rights right now on this
unsuspectible virgin in questions?

But I contain my desirable instinks just long enough to
ask directionals to the john and place a standard FOB COD
reorder on another brewsky, me followin' her tight, shim-
myin', barely covered butt as far as the kitchen door, then turn
left, where I step down Mammory Lane, just past Amnesial
Avenue, where it intersex Forgettin' Bull-o'-vard, 'cause truth
is — and I hate to emit it — that's just where I passed out,
yesterday afternoon, and the missus had to come collect me,
a em-bare-assment o' riches for the boths of us.

But that's just what happened, and I'm damn certain,
havin' had a entire night to sleep it off, finger it out, damn
certain it was them fuckin' TVs, all goin' like Packed-Mans,
eatin' everything in sights, makin' a guy go dizzy just tryin' to
keep up, leapfrog between all them screamin' images 'n neon
lizards 'n frogs 'n stalag-tight spaceships, not to mention all
them young Aztecian 'n Peruvian dropouts not helpin' a guy
like me relax, just chill out on a Sunday afternoon, watchin'
grown adults conduck geniecide on theirselfs, not helpin'
one bit when the one waitin' on me actually rubs up against
my bicep. I mean there's a limit to anyone's constrains, even
if I do call myself a law-abitin', uncivilized citizen, who, most
o' the times, anyways, has got enough self-a-steam for my
wife's right to privacy not to be sneakin' off with some young
thing, even if in my hard I'm sinnin' like a goat in heat,
wantin' to jump 'n hump Fubar's finest.

So now it's Monday, and I'm back on the line, and the only thing I'm screwin' is motor mounts like there ain't no yesterdays nor tomorrows today neither, goin' hellbent for lather, which I'm workin' up like a racedhorse at Pimpleco, knowin' that that sweat's ninety-eight-proof Bud Light, 'til one o' my buddies up the line, Kowalski, reminds me tonight's *Monday Night's Football*, do I want to come over (and bring the missus along too, natch) and make an evenin' of it — helluva match-up between the Baltimore Brown Ravens 'n the St. Louis Cardinal Rams.

So how can I, in my right minds, refuse a invite, 'specially when snacks 'n brewskies is on the house? But just to show I'm a uncivilized sort, I ask can I bring the dip-'n-chip spread (the missus's great at whippin' up that fancy shit — guano-mole 'n cream cheese 'n zoocheeny 'n such). He says, "Hell, no! Just come as you are," and I commence thinkin' that Tuesday should be a doozie, what with us startin' a brand new Saturn model. . . .

Oh, well — this here's a Merica! We're tough sombitches, and it just don't get no better!

Dropping Out:
The Ultimate Therapy

He can't imagine what all the fuss is, these days, over the way New Age gurus pontificate about the two nemeses to human health and sanity — stress and depression — the glut of gut-wrenching confessions and testimonies about everything from physical abuse by au pairs, incest, rape, and sodomy by pederasts, graduate-school pedagogues, and backbiting basketball announcers to the philandering of bombastic presidents parading as the best of the brightest in Come-a-lot, the proliferation of charismatic solutions to America's crisis of spirituality, illuminations of the dark night of the soul through million-print-run paperbacks, as first seen on Oprah's Payola-of-the-Month Book Club.

Where he used to grow dizzy with bewilderment, none of it makes any difference to him anymore. He didn't ream himself from stem to stern with envy, flay his brain with skepticism, anger, or racism, or even get worked up when a recent *Newsweek* cover, displaying the *Mona Lisa* smirk of Deepak Chopra, staring out like a stoned Buddha, arrived and departed inscrutably, with none of its readers the wiser for the feature exposing how this "genius" from India has bought up the Spice Islands in a decade by fleecing American rubes of discretionary rupees they've spent to discover extended immortality as practiced in the Shangri-la of James Hilton, if not in any Tibet known to man.

Nor does he get ripped, bent out of shape when today's snake-oil messiahs witness in tongues, display demonic tendencies beneath their Armani Versaces, promise satori, nirvana, all while being audited by the IRS. He knows true peace of mind comes to those in need when they learn to shed all expectations of success, wealth, position, celebrity, sex, like a bear adapting its heartbeat to a perpetual winter.

Long ago, he disavowed ambition for its own sake, fled
the Garden of Earthy Delights, one night late, with just the
fig leaf on his *schmeckle*, descended into the underbrush
east of lusty Eden, and hid there for ten years in a sleep
those who passed him mistook for meekness. When he fi-
nally awakened, fully clothed in grace, he was so serene that
he went about existence in a nimbus of tranquillity, radical
docility, a cosmic love-pulse matrix, which his family, friends,
business associates, and enemies assumed to be a chronic
state of catatonia, a divine sign or Satanic punishment visited
on him for resigning from life without a fight, a doubt, a sigh.

Junk-Mailed to Death

Just the other day, an inconspicuous piece of bulk-rate mail, the kind that's sent in an unstamped envelope of ghostly slate gray, lacking return address, all reference to sender, even computer-clip-art logo, arrived in your condominium postbox, begged you to throw it in the trash along with coupon "newspapers," fliers, shampoo samples, single-sheet Xeroxed stuffers for real-estate listings, waterproofing companies, and two-for-the-price-of-one "Deep-Dish Combo Meals" from a baker's dozen of local pizza chains, all crammed together like corpses in a catacomb.

Yet, for what impulse you can't say, you hesitated, possibly afraid of discarding a *real* windfall, ran your thumb along its glued flap, resurrected this dead-letter-file item not from oblivion necessarily but silence, its cryptic message brought to life by your curiosity:

"BURIAL PLOTS! MAUSOLEUM CRYPTS!
SACRED SPACES FOR URNS
AND OTHER ASH-BEARING VESSELS
RADICALLY REDUCED, SLASHED TO THE BONE
FOR IMMEDIATE OCCUPANCY — RENT-CONTROLLED —
SALE OF A LIFETIME!"

The announcement, in not-all-together inviting type, with rigid, unpoetic lines advertising B'nai Mount Zion's fire sale, seemed even to you a too-obvious ploy to get a quick cash infusion. (Who would maintain it once all graves were sold?) Ah, and the retail and wholesale prices listed together for convenient comparison shopping — a Kmart blue-light special, a winning Powerball ticket come in, a not-to-be-missed genuine steal, guaranteed limited to the next three weeks, your last chance for a premium nook at bargain-basement savings in a Shurgard U-Store-It Self-Storage for the afterlife.

But the offer imposed two stiff restrictions: to take immediate advantage of such a deal, you had to be a member of a Jewish congregation in St. Louis and you had to purchase, in the mausoleum anyway, two vaults side by side (not necessarily spousal) to keep the wall space in an orderly configuration, like laying tile patterns in a bathroom floor.

You've always thought in terms of keeping dry, safe not just from rain but dogs lifting their legs and kids doing grave-tracings for school projects. But as a bona-fide bachelor, a Jew by birth, if little else, in truth an atheist, you hardly comply with the requirements for buying your final dwelling place at B'nai Mount Zion. Worse, at $75,000 for two (which doesn't include the sealer caskets) — **"AN ADDITIONAL 5% OFF TOTAL FOR PAYMENT UP FRONT!"** — who can afford to die? It's cheaper just to live forever and bury the mail.

Abiogenesis

This Thursday morning, words he'd like to resurrect from the dead, that they might articulate images from his dreams, speak the language of demons still screaming at him in this miasmic mist he locates at the epicenter of waking, so that at least he'd understand his raison d'être, don't materialize. He remains mute, staring laserlike into his breakfast, trying to discern some original significance in the omeletted concoction, but as he descends a Piranesian chain into its steaming cheese-and-onion crater, hoping to reach its base before it erupts in his face, the primordial form of a fly wriggles to the edge of the plate.

Something — an instinct — brings him to his senses. He shudders, alternates between trepidation and disgust, repulsion completely disrupting his equanimity. In the middle of the bustling café, where he comes seven days a week, he mounts the messy table, using his chair as a stepladder, begins shouting in tongues, a hysterical, deranged babble — whinnying, barking, braying, hooting, howling — setting up such a diabolical caterwauling that customers withdraw, like shell-shocked turtles, from cleaning their plates, choke on their omelets, vomit, the place resembling a scene from Dante or Bosch.

He tears off his suit coat, rips tie and shirt from his sweating body, next his shoes, dress pants, boxers, gartered socks, stands as if up to his neck in a stream of red-hot lava, his sounds metamorphosing into horrible grunts, the grunts into moaning, bellowing, wailing, until, in a fit of perfectly lucid jubilation, he catches himself up short, gathers every rational thought into a gall-ball, and spits it at the speechless crowd. It explodes, like a grenade, into word-shrapnel whizzing past or biting them bloody:

"I am Lord of the Flies, Prince of Maggots, burrowing into the anal orifice, up the gut, to the brain, leaving larvae to

multiply in disordered frenzy, eat away all reason for exist-
ence! I am the insect infesting your nightmares, dreams!
Trust me! I am the bug you're to become when you break
from your eggs, into words."

Half-Lives of Postmen, Poets, and Giant Talking Clams

He might have been a postman — must have been — in his last lifetime, because, come acid rain or polluted moonshine, he's up and going at the stroke of midnight, midlife, that mystical moment of metamorphosis when all falls away and dissolves into nostalgia, except his naked soul, stranded out in the middle of a pumpkin patch, trying to find the Catalytic Witch of the Cosmic Abyss, force her to release him from her spell, let him resume his jettisoned dream of one day, one incarnation, becoming something noble and decent and compelling, about whom to write home to Mother Earth, maybe even a poet — preposterous as that might seem — or giant talking clam or sacred, black, opium-smoking orchid of the upper Amazon or gleaming coach-and-four transporting him to a coronation of his spirit, flesh, and bones . . .

Up and going, as if entrusted to deliver the post in Hebron, Watts, Kinshasa, and Abu Dhabi simultaneously, as if the only task that matters, come hellhounds and high red tide, rain-shine, moon-snow, monsoon, tsunami, typhoon, is delivering himself up despite the absence of his bespelled, unholy, incomplete soul — festering in a pumpkin patch, rotting from underneath, being eaten by dung beetles, fire ants, termites, time — which he hopes, at any mystical moment, might return to him as an oracle of the Lord and deliver him from his wicked enchantment, deliver him into safe hands, postman and post of no tangible difference, since his epistle, scripted by himself to himself, was written in disappearing ink . . .

Up and going nonetheless, up and going, up and going . . . going, going, going, going, come you and I and the postman know what.

Upstaged

Needlessly to say, them mackerel snappers 'n fishmon-
grels crouchin' in around the Cathlick table here in Redbird's
like it's a Stupor Bowl huddle 'n them concoctin' up a mother
of all plays to win a losin' battle in the last final seconds with
some stupendulous Heil Mary full o' grease, the fat one, with
the laugh like a cacklin' grackle or five-legged highrena in
heat . . . needlessly to say, theirs is all up in a hornet's nest
o' wasps over what's been transcendin' in the news the past
twenty-eight hours, which is somethin' I never follow too
much, since I can always count on gettin' a shitload of it from
them self-anointed town criers from the Church o' What's
Happenin' Now 'n Then, which, today, amounts to a landfall
o' gossip 'n a toxic-waste dump o' hypolcrisy, or so they say,
me just sittin' here, tryin' to ingest breakfast, mindin' my own
beeswax 'n theirs too, unavoidably, since they got no con-
passion nor sympalthy neither for a guy who done put away
a six-pack o' brewskies in a two-hour dressed rehearsal last
night, tryin' to build up my staminal for this comin' Sunday,
when the Elways 'n the Favors butts heads for the Stupor
Bowl weddin' ring 'n all the gory glory 'n postgame partyin'.
      So I'm just mainlinin' my java to offset the dizzies, a bite
here o' ham-mushedroom-'n-cheese eggs omlit, a bite there
o' double order o' bagel (my buddies at the Saturn factory
over to Fenton swear them bagels is Bible food, unlevanated
'n kosher-pickled or somethin', guaranteed to soak up all
the excessable alcohol drops that might be hangin' over in
the veins, contamilnatin' the normal homogoblins, bring
on instant sobrification, which I'm gonna need in little less
than a hour, when the work bell rings for my shift at the
plant), just chewin' away, mindin' my own beeswax, asbestos
I can, if you catch the drift o' last night's draft I done drunk
from Mr. Anthiser Bush's best bottles o' Light, tryin' to tune
out all that blather 'n word-slop they feed each other each

mornin', not able to keep from listenin' to them discussin' the Pope.

"Hey, boys, you see the Pope over there in Cuba?"

"Yeah, what a clotheshorse Castro is, huh?"

"Yeah, he cuts quite a figure in that three-piecer of his."

"First one in forty years, I bet!"

"First one since his bar mitzvah in the fifties!"

"Jesus, wouldn't you think he'd have worn those army fatigues and that Afro-scraggly beard to greet the Holy Father?"

"Give the guy some credit, boys. At least he sees a good thing when it's there — a chance to legitimately lambaste the U.S. for committing genocide by keeping the trade embargo going."

"Yeah, he's putting the pressure on good old Uncle Sam, sure enough."

"Pontiff's being there to bless the people makes us look real bad by default or proxy or something, like that scruffy Bluebeard's some sort of a saint or martyr for suffering the little babies to know hunger."

"Yeah, but the upshot was on Ted Koppel last night."

At this point o' no returns, I almost choke on a chunk o' bagel, tryin' to stomach their apple-pieousness, one o' them narratin' how Tom Cobbler o' *Nightlife* was sayin' how he intended to be alive from Cabana, but then they got the late-breakin' news about Clinton, and new shenanigans came to life that made the whole crew pull up tent stakes and set up their three-ring circus back to the Beltloop.

"Can you imagine anyone on the planet, short of God Himself, upstaging His Regal Holy Father, the Pontiff and Pope? Jesus, what an insult!"

And me realizin', now that I look up, that Redbird's is a bumblerbee's nest o' gossip, a-whisperin' 'n a-buzzin' goin' on, and each mouth's got the same pollen on its lips, that sweet honey from all Clinton's honeypots, and now I'm thinkin', why in hell does all this stuff matter, since all us guys, by our musculine natures, is prone to gettin' in double-

dutch apples with the more fairer sex, just 'cause man's
always done it since Atom gave the go-ahead, green-light high
sign. Well, I don't really know for sure if he cheated on his
old lady, Eve, mistress or whatever she was — temptress,
slut, bimbo, I'd say, to be perfectly unbiassed — God only
knows . . . maybe.

But, truth is, one way nor the other three, this bucket the
Prez done stuck his foot in headfirst into ain't no great
shakes. It goes on all the time, even among presildents —
imagine how many Castrate's had on his Castrol convertibles
'n Sadman Insane 'n Q.T.'s Botive over there in Afurca. I
mean, come on, what's the big deal here? Even I done it on
my wife when I knew I could get away with it, just by takin'
sick leave for lunch to Q.T.'s, with no one the wisest about
me makin' side deals with them babes dancin' on my laptop,
nekkid as *Penthorse* centerfoals in their birthday suits and a
helluva lot more interested in my cat-o'-nine-tails, me lickin'
the best breasts in town for lunch! Jesus, if your old lady
was as porky as mine or as ugly a bitch as Hillary (a real ball-
buster from the word go-nad, guarangoddamnteeya!), and, in
his case — the Prez's, that is — poor bastard, with a daughter
that looks like they made her outten Play-Doe or Silly Putny
'n put her in a vice or C-clamp 'n squeezed to beat all shit, then
who's to say what length a guy might not go to just to protect his
sanity 'n his faith in beautitude, not to mention his manhoods?

"Boys, can you believe what this womanizer's done now?
They can't get him on fornicating on the job, but they can cut
his nuts off, impeach him for perjury, getting that Jew girl,
Lewinsky, to lie under oath."

"Yeah, he's in deep shit, up to his hips in alligators now,
I'd say, what with Paula Jones in one pocket and now this one
in the other."

"A hell of a game of pocket pool, I'd say!"

"Yeah, and he's the eight ball in both side pockets!"

"Yeah, but what jerks my knee is how he's usurped the
Pope. There must be some divine justice in this whole mess."

And me thinkin' them mongrel snappers is just bein' sour lemon balls, bad sports who quit when the wind changes 'n the goin' gets so tough they can't tell their asses from Asstroturf, and the great lawn mower in the sky's about ready to cut their grass to a crisp, pissed 'cause their big guy got the short-order shrift, had all the wind knocked outten his sails 'n unflated with still air. I mean, it ain't every day that a pope gets invited by a eggnostic atheist undisbeliever, like Infidel Castrate, to come to his cuntry to spread the Gospull 'n the Words to a pack o' cigar-chompin', sugarcane-choppin' unexcommunicable heathens, only to have all that beeswax blow up in their faces, gone with the winds, forgot on the spot, have all the news-median troops brought home to focus on a Prez's nocturnal admissions to the White House.

"So, as I say, Clinton's in it up to his ears this time, and I, for one, hope they stick it to him good, make him drop his pants, unfurl his johnson, and wave it like Old Glory, show his stars and stripes for Paula Jones to identify up close and personal!"

"Maybe then he can go home to Little Rock and sit up on a high bluff overlooking Whitewater, yodeling or singing the good-ol'-boy blues or crooning 'Camptown Ladies' or 'Mister Bojangles' in a minstrel-show chorus with Vernon Jordan!"

"Yeah, maybe he can go on an Easter-egg hunt for the bones of Vince Foster!"

"And maybe he can get Gennifer Flowers's unlisted number and get a blind date with her roommate!"

"And maybe he can invite Jim Guy Tucker, Dick Morris, Web Hubbell, and Jodie Foster over for the Super Bowl and have an all-day game of strip poker with the ladies from the Beardstown Travel Office!"

And them goin' on like this shit's the funniest shit to hit the fan in a coon's age, and me tryin' to finger out why so many people, politicals 'n religional fantastics alike, like them holier'n-thou guys over to the Cathlick table, why all they seem to got on their minds is the sleaze, the "tabloidal mantality," as I call it, why they all seem to think it's always the other guy who's gotta be squeakin' clean even if they ain't.

Truth is, I bet to hell even Pope Pilate's gone a few rounds in the ring, done the rope-a-dope with a none or three nor eight, hidin' in one o' them tunnels connectin' his chambers 'n pots 'n such with them special chapels underneath the Fattycan, where they perform them sacrifacial rights 'n wrongs, if you know what I mean, catch the drift o' my Popal bull.

Trapped at the Gasworks

For the past six months, he's been conspicuously af-flicted with flatulence. It seemingly arrived out of the clear blue sky, like a Biblical plague of grasshoppers blinding Pharaoh's eye to the future with its pervasive rapaciousness, just as this has done to him, keeping him in a constant state of vigilance to avoid the embarrassing passings of gas that escape without a smidgen of warning ("Har*ass* my ass," as he phrases it to his cronies), those insidious breakings of wind that a confusion of pills in his stomach's bat cave send blast-ing, by mistake, into the light of day, the mixture wreaking havoc on his enzymes, causing Hiroshimas and Nagasakis around the clock.

And he "can't do shit about it," he's confessed to his gastroenterologist, his cardiologist, his perplexed HMO G.P. Neither he nor they suspect it's the conflictive pills conspir-ing to lay on him a debilitating philter. The best remedy, the most sage advice, his Smith Brothers cough-drop doctors can possibly conjure consists simply of his eating a Third World diet of bread and water, rice, potatoes, and fish, taking an oc-casional cup of decaffeinated tea as a placebo-reward for his abstemious good behavior. And this he's complied with rigidly, until he's gotten so sick of three squares of prison fare and his gesture to British civility/faggotry, he's now vow-ing to cut out his large and small intestines.

"How can they expect this piss to calm an upset gut?" he grumbles, sipping his Red Zinger tea at the Eat-Rite. "With this compost heap of mine, I wouldn't be surprised if feed-ing it these ingredients — hibiscus petals, rose hips, roasted chicory and licorice root, lemon grass, lemon verbena, lemon horseshit — isn't the equivalent of lions serving the starved Romans their Christian, Jew, pagan, and heathen leftovers."

No sooner does he finish fulminating than he shatters a lusty bottle of bubbly on the prow of a massive fart poised in its scaffolding, sends it sliding down its rectal bedways. The entire café is stunned, chokes, then dies of shell-shock paroxysm and asphyxia seizure, abandoning him in the killing fields of holistic medicine.

Space Traveler

What a sad little bastard he is — fifty-six years ragged and not three pennies in his piggy bank, an earthly estate that would make a gutter-bum kneel and give thanks to God for his own good fortune before taking another swig from his perpetual fifth.

It wasn't always this way. He can still recall his youthful promise, the academic and athletic records he set in high school and college, graduate-class awards he won on his way to becoming the youngest MBA in the program, his meteoric ascendancy to CEO of one of St. Louis's most prestigious corporations by the time he was thirty.

Wow! Those were the fast-paced days, all right, like a hockey match on and off the ice. He had it all, in that stellar decade when he moved his company from his basement office to a skyscraper at Eighth and Washington, his personality a giant white star pulling all swirling galactic matter into the vortex of his ambition and conditional love, absorbing their force, adding it to his own: submissive wife, beautiful, dutiful children, extended family, friends, business and social associates, every known essence approaching his orb forever transformed into emanations from his core . . .

Until, one day, he awoke and it was over, the brainstorms, those explosions of genius that peers and elders rewarded with esteem and wealth, that infectious laughter, that cosmic energy, which for ten years had fathered novas, quasars, given birth to stars far and near, flaring and pulsating, illuminating his deep universe, over in a flash, a reversed big bang, in an astrological manner of speaking, galaxies colliding in inner space, his psychic workings rolling back over him, flattening him beneath their retreating light waves, creating cognitive meltdown, a depression the breadth and depth of his helplessness.

For seven years, he remained in total isolation, sequestered in a "rest home," whose expenses eventually drained his resources, drove his family into destitution, diminished him to a drug-addicted jellyfish, a wunderkind reduced to gutless wonder by the time the administrators at Arsenal Street determined he could be released on his own Thorazine-and-Zoloft recognizance. He left the asylum with the shirt on his back, one change of underwear issued him from the stockroom, and the mandatory hundred dollars and one cent, fulfilling the state's obligation, and set off in quest of a halfway house close by.

These days, if he could, he'd analogize his existence to a piece of space junk, a defunct satellite, module floating aimlessly through the heavens. In truth, his missions vary from useless to futile. He's a fixture few St. Louisans recognize, though they drive past his tatterdemalion shadow ever probing downtown trash cans, garbage bags stacked in alleys behind restaurants, rifling reeking dumpsters, in which he sleeps on freezing nights, otherwise in office doorways, between cardboard sheets. He goes about his derelict business in succinct silence, disturbs the universe barely an iota.

Keeping an Eye on Things

Beware!

Beware the colossal eye in the sky! God is watching on High from somewhere, anywhere, everywhere, *urbi et orbi* simultaneously, and if not God, then it's got to be Hieronymus Bosch, hiding behind the iris or inside the pupil of a gigantic painted conceit of his, hanging in the bedroom of Philip II of Spain, staring apocalyptically into his dreams, repeating subliminally, through REM-visions,

Beware of the one-eyed Union Jack, the two-legged jack-off-all-trades, six-packs of Cracker Jack snacks, immaculate deceptions, and three-legged Labyrinths toppled off their pedestals in the valley of Ozymandias, whose sneers of cold command and sandy despair can make a man defecate in his arrogant pants just for daring to rub those stony noses, still cold and wet as a pharaoh hound's ten centuries after its master decapitated, flayed, and ate it during the Dark Ages to prove that he who lies down with and lays canines wakes up fleeing trypanosome sleeping disease!

Beware of Trafalgar Square, Rumpelmayer's, Stuckey's, Horn & Hardart's!

Beware of pregnant Greeks bearing Trojan horses instead of courageous soldiers, delivering up their foals through Cesarean section — eight-legged, all-terrain Sleipnir, Clever Hans, Whirlaway, Al Borak, Houyhnhnms, Francis "The Talking Ford" Coppola, a.k.a. Henry "The Anti-Semite" Ford Coprophiliac, S.A.!

Beware of cyclopean Dale Chihuly tonguing his phallic blowpipe, using his sperm as molten gob, which he metamorphoses into giant glass clams with electric-eel lip-wraps that cause financial lockjaw to true believers of the arts-'n-crafts cross!

And if it turns out not to be good ol' buddy Hieronymus "Buford" Lily-white Pusser, founder of the Fetid Society of

Nazi Fetal-Pig-People, that wonderful Wizard of Ozymandias, then it can only be Prince Lucifer of Worms, the worm in the apple of God's Eye, good ol' Bud Light, *"lux et veritas,"* star of *Days of Our Lies*, socially entropic in his philanthropic misanthropy despite his legendary perversions of the truth, that Angel of the Celestial Camps, Dr. Mangley of the Dangling Dingleberry, Butcher of Bedlam, Panderer of Pandemonium, Pederast of Phlegethon and Lake Woebegone, man of the year in Hayward, Hurley, and Hell, the boy king Too-tanked-too-often, of the realms of Punxsutawney and Piscataway, the man most likely to succeed himself when all hell breaks loose and the heavens open up with thunderous clap and AIDS and the skies send great-flaming *Challenger*s earthward, screaming bodies of gaseous incandescence (super-heated globs of Chihuly-like sea foam) that appear to be the blinking eyes of gargantuan cuttlefish to the naked human eye staring up out of beds sumptuously ensconced in a million palatial chambers in New Madrid, Missouri, and Toledo, Ohio, beds soiled by incontinent Prince Philip Feigenbaums of Jewish-Christian Rainbow-Coalition Inquisitions.

Beware of fallen angels, space-junk sputniks falling helter-skelter like guillotine blades, severing heads of state!

Beware the colossal eye in the sky, that omniscient petri dish of deadly anthrax, watching over us with the focus of a Hubble telescope, fitted out with a Hieronymus Bosch & Lomb lens, at once convex and concave, inspecting our most minute perfections and blemishes as though tomorrow and yesterday were a blink of the Almighty eye, which, at any gratuitous moment, might shut for good!

"Making Chicken Salad Out of Chicken Shit": A Foreword by A. Colonel Lingus, to *So You'd Like to Try Your Hand at Writing for a Living*, by Executive Sous-Chef Hosea "Butch" Butcher of Lyons, Georgia

By now, he's actually forgotten who first assigned him to grinding out words, stuffing wads at a time into his mind-grinder, cranking its ball-point-pen handle like a man possessed, until they squeeze through millions of miles of conduits — raw-edged neurons greased with electrical impulses — and reach the bottom of the discharge tube, passing through holes that shape them into fine strands he can place on freezer paper, wrap, and preserve in time's meat locker. His favorite preparation is ground-round-brains tartar.

He can't recall who initiated him into this business, when he switched from chicken to red meat, learned to butcher whole sides of beast — horse, jackass, llama, and giraffe — render from centaur, gorgon, griffin, chimera cuts appetizing enough to pass regal muster, create novel uses for previously scorned organs; he's even thrown in snoods, sagittal crests, and horns, foreskins and phalluses from tapirs, unicorns, North Sea walruses, and Zipperrumpazoos, vaginas from Greek sirens no longer in vogue.

Some critics have deemed him a haute-cuisine genius. The President has proclaimed him a national treasure, twice invited him to the White House to prepare his inaugural addresses for public consumption. He's been told he's the masses' darling, that they await each of his words with bated breath, eat them up with gusto bordering on piranha feed-

ing-frenzies. The chains can't keep his cookbooks in stock.
(His latest is Oprah's selection of the month: *Forty Ways to
Serve Purple-Throated Bombast for Xmas*; it's been moving
like shit through a Christmas goose.)

These days, he neglects his Manhattan rendering plant/
bistro, spends days staring out of his Sherry-Netherland pent-
house, dazed by his success, intoxicated by his celebrity,
especially when he remembers that a mere ten years ago, he
was cleaving chicken wings, thighs, breasts, drumsticks in
the Tyson fowl facility in Lyons, Georgia, working for chicken
feed, until that revelatory morning when, bored, he turned a
gizzard into a Petrarchan sonnet, a neck into a *New Yorker*
short story, and knew his future was all cock-and-bull-a-
doodle-do.

Iced Ages

Strange how you can think about somethin' so hard it gets stuck in your brain like a too-big chunk o' chewy rib-eye in the throat. Be damned if that ain't what happened last night. The old lady kept pushin' 'n shovin' me all night long, tryin' to get me to quit kickin' 'n thrashin' in bed.

Actually, in fack, unbeknowin'ly to her, the mattress was a ménage à twat o' three ladies o' the night I was humpin' in my dreams. I guess it musta felt pretty damn good, too, 'cause I near to busted the fuckin' boxed springs, what with my Olympian-gold-metal dolffin stroke goin' like a mother through that pool o' dreams, which seemed like three oceans hooked to each other long.

Jeezus! I didn't even know, 'til the bell done clung at 4 a.m., that I was so wrung out — not my 'jamas, 'cause I ain't never wore none, but the sheets 'n blankets 'n the missus's gown, which might as well be Omar the Tentmaker's latest, his new Ring-a-Ling Brothers Barnacle Bill Bailey big top, considerin' you can't mistake my old lady for Cindy Crawdad nor one o' them *Penthorse* centerfoals exackly neither . . .

But as I say, I musta give that bed its money's worth, what with humpin' it like a mad freak. Truth is, I can see now, more clearlier'n mud, that what I was up to was bein' massively horny, sufferin' a midnight Mac attack o' nocturnal admissions, what for havin' spent too much wasted energy yesterday listenin' to them bastard mackerel snappers at Redbird's fart-baggin' about ol' Jefferson Bill Clinton 'n his hairem of underagers, then, on top o' that, so to speak, havin' to indure precisely the same identical shoptalk (the factory guys was buzzin' up a sandstorm, like someone done dropped a ton o' truth syrup on the Ding Dongs 'n Fruit Rolled-Ups in their lunchbuckets) about the Prez's pension for reality-checkin' his dipstick, creatin' his own Monastery o' the Interior right there in the White House pool, doin' all his straddlegizin' with his other head o' state, apparently gettin' it on with any- 'n everything that moves, 'cept maybe his wife, that nut-buster of all mothers, and me thinkin' how it's already been at least two days since I got my last piece off the old lady (what with her complainin' o' the minstrel red tide or gas or that oldest o' femalian standbys, the multigrain head-snake, all 'n any o' which she wheels out on a ass-needed, first-come, first-serviced bases, dependin' on whether her mood's barometer-fallin' or -risin', sleet nor slush comin' in on the next Ardick air mast or El Nemo hisself, bringin' in the gangreenhouse affect o' rain-forest breezes from the Far Tartufos or Madagascan) or a bodacious fuck in the kitchen, on the spot, unannounced, orgaseous as the La Brean tar-pots bubblin' like Ol' Faithless, if you catch the thrust o' my spray.

I mean, you can't never tell when she's gonna just wanna up 'n jump your bones right there in the Kotexass aisle o' Wal-Fart or at the dessert bar in Pounderosa. (I always go back for sloppy seconds on the softy-cream!) You know women — one minute, they're complainin' o' bein' abused 'n antifeminized 'n her-assed; the next, they got their hot, wet lips around your dick-head without you even knowin' how they Houdinied your weenie right outten its ziplick bag. I mean, unpredicktable — I guess!

Anyways, the point is I'm exhausted this mornin', too tired to even listen to them Cathlicks go at it again, rehash the same ol' Dinty Moore, since the Prez ain't playin' out too many o' his racial cards ('cept if you consider his ace o' spades in the hole, Vermin Jordan), not at least 'til his tamers 'n personal trainers 'n spin witch doctors 'n attorneys to law can get a grip on his story between the lines nor the bed-sheets nor whatever. And truth be known, I couldn't give two shits in Chinatown . . . or could I?

That bad sleep last night — I know what it was now, and I'm thinkin' that, come noon, I just better contrack one o' them migratory headsnakes, blamin' my old lady for a communicative disease, get good ol' Alferneeze, the line boss, to grant me sick lunch leave, a extra two hours to recupinate 'n sneak on downtown, 'crost the river, to Q.T.'s, get a quick fix o' some lap lunch, a few o' Kernel Lingus's best finger-lickin' breasts o' breast, if you catch my presildental drift.

After all, it ain't exackly quite fair for Bill Clinton to have to evoke executed privileges every time he needs to get a little nookie on the side for sufferin' perpetual vapor lock from the First Old Lady and for the rest of us ordinary Jobs, who just happen to be keepin' the economies humpin' right along, not to be able to consider the Prez a rolled model o' good ethnics 'n amorality. It may be a dog-eat-pussy world, but it's also a zoo out there, and when it comes to minkey see, minkey doo-doo, I'm all for the inequality of all democratic parties.

I mean, it's just that simple. I went to bed last night, in good faiths, actually feelin' sorry for the Presildent, him bein' accused o' bein' a womanizer 'n sleazebag, actually empal-thizin' with him, thinkin' how he'd be gettin' into bed be-sides that bitch in his Lincoln Log Bed in their Offal Office bedroom, just like me gettin' in besides my helpmeat, knowin' that neither him nor me is gonna get any tonight for vari-ous similarities o' differin' conditions, Bill 'n me bein' in the same bed, so to speak, in the same barrel-boat, high 'n dry dock, shut off for good-only-knows how long it'll take him to work his way outten this croaker sack 'n me 'til I happen to catch my old lady either needin' somethin' outten me, like a new Hoover, nor forgettin' she ain't really menopausa-tional after all.

Whatever, I bet Bill was dry-humpin' his bed last night too. I tell you, this gettin' shut off, what with so much pres-sure on us guys to bring home the cold cuts 'n brewskies, can drive a guy to a Hillary Flower or Paula Lipinsky or, in my case, a little afternoon delight over to Q.T.'s or one o' them other sportin' bars over to Sauget.

Face it, it don't make no difference whether you're Brett

Elway, Jefferson Bill Clinton, or me, myselfs, 'n I; a man's
gotta be able to get 'em off if he's gonna get it on, if you
acquire the drift o' my draft — and that don't mean onced
every other iced ages nor eight!

Homo oneiricus

His dreams seem astonishingly atavistic to him, riddled with classic characteristics suggesting that, millions of years ago, he, his primordial spirit, anyway, participated in that ongoing battle royal between mammals and reptiles, his essence once shaped like a gorilla or mandrill, if not considerably more devolved along the chain of being, in the form of a dinosaur or other prelapsarian beast; he may have even been the Komodo dragon's predecessor.

In any event, his evolutionary dreams are perpetually assailed by scaly snakes, snakes rarely, if ever, symbolic, metaphoric — in other words, not Satanic serpents lurking in Eden's purlieus but actual rattlesnakes, moccasins, hissing cobras, pythons, and boa constrictors — and nightly, he finds himself wide awake in his nightmares, transported to a REM rain forest, where his greatest fear, besides dying in his sleep, is falling from his arboreal nest, crashing to the floor, into a pit of seething vipers, which have no penile or clitoral connection to sex despite erections he sprouts like weeds when deeply engorged in his oneiric phobias, all of which evokes some Cenozoic ape or monkey he must have once been, in those dim days before he developed an enlarged brain cage containing sophisticated neocortical equipment, which, to this day, lets him imagine, abstract independently, and extrapolate from all data the Internet feeds him that he too is a species on the verge of extinction, just another higher primate in a zoo, terrified of his slithering, venomous shadow, of falling from grace.

Veteran Doorman

So tumultuous is this early-morning rain that it drives straight through the oversize umbrella he opens against the tempest, as though its taut skin were cheesecloth, pervious to the hallucinatory gray sheets that transport his damp spirit back to Vietnam, back to the perpetually wet Mekong Delta, back to 1971, late in the game.

Outfitted in doorman's uniform with shiny, vinyl-billed cap and patent-leather shoes, matching blue epauletted jacket and striped pants, he escorts the building's residents from the lobby, beyond the canopy, to their cars, keeps them from getting drenched — protects them from stepping on land mines, being shot by sniper fire, grenaded, napalmed.

He takes his responsibilities seriously. It's just that on stormy days like this, when traffic hissing past on the boulevard sets up a sinister mist and rain shows no mercy for anyone's mission, for reasons not altogether scrutable to him, he's thrust back into that shuddering Chinook carrying forty of his platoon buddies, cast into that three-hundred-foot vertical crash, from which fewer than half of them would be worth evacuating to field hospitals for bullet and shrapnel wounds, flesh burned to festering — maggots' feast.

He takes his job seriously, indeed, does fine until a deluge like this slips through repression's fragile nets and he's huddling in those muddy bunkers, choking on soggy C rations, uniform saturated, leather boots growing green mold — soaked to the bone for a year . . . until he loses control of his inundated mind, bares his soul to the residents, mutters about the gooks, Khmer Rouge, McNamara, eight-year-old "friendlies" by day, enemies by night . . . until, after assisting Mrs. Stevens, he depresses the release on his umbrella, draws it into a tight rifle, his trusty M-16, instinctively scans the driveway for signs of mines, then sights along the barrel, carefully takes aim, and begins firing like crazy at all the Vietcong driving on Hanley Road in the rain.

Roswell

Somethin' fell over Roswell, New Mexico, in the summer of '47, damn sure, 'cause it fell in my field, scattered all to hell, in little pieces that looked like balsa wood and others that resembled tinfoil.

Air Force sent a few people to collect up the mess, haul it off in a truck to the base, sent out a "public-relations officer" sayin' it was some kind of alien vehicle, one of them Flash Gordon/Buck Rogers contraptions — you know, spaceships, flyin' disks — and this guy Marcel puts out a news release that gets picked up in the *San Francisco Chronicle*, *Washington Post*, and London *Times*, till, on a thin dime, Air Force does a 180-degree about-face, says the wreckage ain't what they said, instead's a experimental, high-altitude weather balloon that got popped by a passin' pigeon.

And that was s'posed to shut up the skeptics, which it all but did. And who was I to disagree with higher-ups, 'specially since it didn't make me no difference to start with, anyway, 'cept for that stuff gettin' in the path of my tractor?

But truth is, I gotta admit, there was *somethin'* fishy goin' on that week, some kind of shenanigans, them makin' such a fuss over that crash, and then that black rubbery stuff, melted all over the place — felt real strange, almost furry, to the touch. Ain't seen nothin' like that since — almost seemed to be vibratin', like hardened lava that's still flowin'.

Prince Metaphor,
Archenemy of I-Am-Me

I am the Invincible Armada, come a cropper at the hands
of a navy made up of Old Bailey Union Jackoff rejects, floating
off on a sea of Baileys Irish Cream;

I am Mayonnaise, of *The Dirty Dozen* fame, poised to part
Colonel Klink from his scalp in his castle bunker at Wounded
Knee, Germany;

I am a tumescent clitoris protruding from Egon Schiele's
transsexual pudendum;

I am Betty Crocker in Aunt Jemima's apron, Al Jolson in
Jackie "Bojangles" Robinson's face, hiding behind his ebony
shoeshine polish;

I am the Prince of Toads, warts and all, the one who hung
the moon for Cinder-Ella Fitzgerald; I'm the one-armed
paperhanger, Hangman to His Majesty Torquemada and the
Exalted Grand Dragon of the Nathan Bedford Falls Rain-
Forrest Clavern of Flat River, Missouri;

I am the Ritz, Mae West's inflatable tits, the Mount of Olives
mounting the Temple Mount, Chief Be-All-and-End-All of the
last Mohicans, the berries, the cat's meow, Joe Camel's last straw;

I am Uncle Remus's slave, Joel Chandler Harris, chowing
down on rare Brer rarebit in the brier patch, or Mohandas
Gandhi chewing on the sacred cow of Cowcutta, or Ted
Geisel, from La Jolla-upon-Oxnard, feasting at Seder on six
kosher Swomee-Swans, five Humming-Fish, four Brown Bar-
ba-loots, three Truffula Tree tufts, two Loraxes, and a Once-
ler from Once-upon-a-Seuss;

I am a Magna à la Carta cum laude, a Declaration of
Codependence, a Gettysburg Address by Ursula Andress,
Martin Luther King's Ninety-five Feces scotch-taped to the
Birmingham jail's crapper walls, hard-core movable porn hot
off Gutenberg's press;

I am a bird feeder, kitty litter, rubber dog shit and Ham
for Lunch fake barf, Whoopie Goldberg's hissing whoopee
cushion;

I am Mrs. Paul's frozen fish sticks sizzling, St. Paul's
freeze-dried Jesus jerky, cream-of-tartar-sauce toothpaste for
sharks, tall, Jolly Green Hefty trash bags (economy-size box);

I am Tampax, a fax machine, a laxative, a rancid Hollandaise
suppository;

I am the expository epitome of empty epistolary epipha-
nies, my inner ears' sympathetic vibrations, Lady Madonna's
dildo, her compromised hymen, and sweet baby Christ suck-
ling his thumb;

I am a riot, a piece of work, a stitch, a hoot, fit to be tied,
a kick in the pants, a pain in the ass, a hit and a miss, a mess;

I am the best and the worst, a knocked-up-wurst, a Jeffrey
Dahmerstrami sandwich with sordid relishes, the sweaty,
worsted-wool jockstrap of a wasted "Jersey Joe" Walcott,
Madame Louisa May Alcott instructing her promiscuous lit-
tle street-women how to fish out their diaphragms, Reichs-
feldmarschall Marge Schott *Heil*-fiving her Cincinnati Reds
Brownshirts as they hit the "showers";

I am, as I've already confessed, Mayonnaise, as well as
Colonel Mustard and Professor Plum with Spanish fly in the
library, a rope and a lead-pipe cinch in the toolshed, the
Grinch who stole Christmas from Bob Crapshoot's crutch-
wielding son, Tiny Limb, the ape lady Zamorra gone apeshit
in Gomorrah, a Houyhnhnm's horse — of course, of course;

I am *am* in all its wasness and will-be-ing;

I am present and past perfect, imperfectly;

I am subjunctivitis, conditionally;

I am *could* and *would* and *should be* and *were*;

I am *might* and *may be*, maybe;

I am *shall* Silverstein and *will* Shakespeare;

I am tense, tenses, live high-tension wires, Alfred, Lord
Anyone-for-Tennyson, San Francisco's Tenderloin, grilled in
a New York minute;

I am three Egg Beaters and a toasted bagel (please hold the lox and cream cheese, please), breakfast's Bad Boy, Hong Kong "bird flu" pecking out of its shells;

I am the well-hung wurst of times, the breast of times, from Charlie Dick-ins's *A Sale of Two Titties*;

I am sick of being everything to everyone, everyone but myself, that is, just one metastasizing metaphor of misplaced ego-identity, a deformed, disoriented figure of speech, an author in search of his character actors, their stage, his bit-part players, his main man, main squeeze, mainframe, cocaine in the main vein, "insane in the membrane";

I am, as of this pen-stroke, a lease, a subcontract, third mortgage, mechanic's lien rendered null and void, paid-in-full; as of this January, Anno Dominoes 1998, I am neither more nor less than metaphor-free but rather completely disaffiliated, disfranchised, discharged of responsibilities, a fella without magnetic properties, no lodestones in his gonads, blackballed by his multiple personalities, incapable of making links, philosophical copulations, docking at brain-stations in inner space.

Metaphor and I no longer see eye to eye, tongue to penis to vagina, idea to image, sound to silence — oh, no, not I, and not me either.

As of right this minute, I abdicate my throne in the soul's latrine, refuse to be the dumb King of Cum, cream of some young guy's fortune cookie, Winnie Mandela's whipping boy, rather proclaim myself no-load *contendere*, *non* compost praying-mantis *mentis*, not chopped liver or the emperor's new Thneeds, not Zorba the Greek in Victor Manure's sheep's clothes, not the Invisible Armada of 1588, not Grey Poop-on or the Hell Man's "heart-lite" mayonnaise, not Chuck Bronson or Telly Savalas, of Auschwitz-am-Maim fame.

Uh-oh, there I go again! Damn those pesky *I am*s! I am me alone, me only, the one and only me! "Me" is the only syllable of metaphor I'll own.

In Effigy

Once, and for many decades, they said of him behind his back (and to his face) that he cast a wide net in his affairs of state and the heart — a shuttle diplomat to Nefarious, swashbuckling Valentino, torrid Lothario — and projected an enviable record of social successes, while losing few contests against Persephone or the devil, salacious foes posing as worthy opponents.

What a guy! What a guy he was! Nothing about his performances smacked of Walter Mitty or Bartleby the Scrivener. Oh, no! He was a mensch for all seasons, a wizard at extricating himself from tight spots, a knight in not-quite-shining armor, the original fight-or-flight trader in adrenaline futures, who made a killing in a field of vipers and retired at the ripe young age of thirty-five.

Despite his absence, the market went on and, within a matter of months, forgot to honor his inconspicuousness. Others, who, as somewhat less efficient, dexterous, underhanded, manipulative, evil upstarts, had aspired to his heights when he ran roughshod over their lot of young, trigger-happy barbarians, accumulating notches on lust's and greed's pistol butts, soon assumed his stature.

One day, to his dismay, he discovered his wealth, power, and good looks had disappeared. The vanity mirror, that crystal ball he'd consulted for years, refused to reciprocate his wooing. Frantic, he tried to reinstate his claims, but his former underlings and harems pelted him with rocks, crowned him laughingstock, stretched his shriveled net around his body, and hung him upside down from a Mussolini tree to rot.

Q.T.'s in a Pinch

Sure as a owl can see its own shadow in the dark and scare hisself into action, hootin' from fear o' hisself, that's just what I done, come lunchtime, got up the gumptions, that is, to get up off my dead butt and head for my truck. Bell no more than done rung 'til I confronts our line boss, Alferneeze Johnson. (Yeah, these days o' Confirmative Reaction, anyone can astride to the a Merican dream 'n secede, if you know what I mean, catch the degree o' my drift. Thing I'll never understand, none the more nor less, is how them nigs dream up them weird names they give their kids. Like take Alferneeze, just for a example — what in hell is a Alferneeze? Sounds like about half a zillion termhites, all crawlin' around inside the woodworks o' my house, eatin' me outten house 'n hold, so to speak, and for that matter, can you imagine a last name like Johnson? Only Johnson I know intilmately is the well-hung unit dancin' around in my pants, my major crowbar, the one that separates the men from the fagnits, the fagnits from the girls, the tool I use to pry open gift boxes too tight to prize open by hand . . . but I'm regressin'.)

So I tell Alferneeze "Geez, Can't See Ma Knees" Johnson I got one helluva multigrainer (he's familiar with my unhealthy record, my absentitis), need a few hours to air it out, so to speak, let the demons quietin' down, the prairie fire die down to a roar, and he sympalthizes with me, or if he don't, he don't let on that he's done got wind o' just what he can prob'ly tell from my eager eyes is on my minds.

So I screech off the lot, floor it east on 44, all the way to 55, downtown, 'crost the bridge, to that familiar 3 South sign and on into scenic Sauget, groin-pit of a Merica 'n the globular village, what with all its belchin' chemistry companies, all o' which takes me only half the hour it normally takes if a person ain't in a hurry to commit suicide.

And I gotta emit, my veins is filled with odrenalin 'stead

o' blood. My johnson feels like it's a Locked Nest monster
swimmin' around in that New York City sewer system o'
mine, tryin' to find a manhole (or somethin' slightly more ef-
feminal) to pop outten into the lights o' day, which is what
happens soon's I arrive, enter Q.T.'s Adult Entertainment
Complex, 'cause one o' them dancin' babes is greetin' payin'
customers, standin' in front o' the counter, sayin' her hellos
in that universal mother tongue that don't need no trans-
latin', her with absolutely nothin' coverin' herselfs 'cept the
briefest suggestion of a G-string and me wishin' I was a
Germanic symphonial composter, like Beat-Often Bach von
Johnson, to compress 'n dedicate to her my concert in G-
string miner, to be played by my hunnerd-piece orchestral,
made up o' bonophones, skin flutes, tromboners, 'n upright
meat organs — no strings attached. Can you imagine bein'
escorted to your seat by a nekkid babe? And me thinkin', life
is good, thinkin', is this a great cuntry or what?

So I get seated in my own private seat 'n realize, before
I can even get outten my coat, I'm surrounded by six more
babes just as nekkid, all coagulatin' 'n grindin' up on their
own stages. And what with the stutterin' lights, bumpin' mu-
sics, 'n all this flesh with nothin' between them 'n me but
them high-heel pumpers 'n a Band-Aid between their buns
'n almost not coverin' their pussies, I'm turnin' into a volcano
crockedpot o' Mexical jumpin' beans. I flag down a passin'
fancy in skimpy pants 'n top and order three brewskies to
onced, if not sooner, which she brings in a flash 'n a jiffy
from outten thinned air, which takes some o' the pressures
off me, cools my radiator way down soon's I park away one,
then two, bottles in short order, like a genie disappearin' into
his own wish.

And I got my eye on three o' them babes all to onced at
the same time, all humpin' their stages on their stomachs like
somethin' outten a Korean flea circus or a bunch o' swami
wrestlers thumpin' around in their throngs, the most beaute-
ous ladies o' the evenin' 'n afternoon I ever seen to onced,

in one place at the same times.

So when the set finishes, and after I hail a fancy passin' taxi to bring me three more brewskies on the run, I wave a pair o' Washingtonians in the air. It's like baitin' a hook with a worm, knowin' the pond you're fishin's been stocked with keepers; only, in this case, the worm's my major player, the ol' one-eyed trouser worm, my night crawler, the ol' striped garter grub, and the keepers is all temporary 'n not permanel, gets throwed back, 'cause them's the rules in this joint, to keep guys like me from ruinin' the merchantdice, bruisin' the fresh fruit, filetin' the fish to the bone — *my* bone, in this case, if you catch my catch-o'-the-day drift.

Before I know it, a struttin' slut who just finished her theater-in-the-around comes swimmin' up to grab them two ones off my hook. Before I know what's bitten my bait, I got her smooth, ripe guavas — honeydews with their rhines removed, more like it — swingin' 'n slappin' back 'n froth acrost my lips, askin' me to taste o' her fruit's cocktail, which I do without thinkin' two times about it, my tongue speakin' in tongues for all they're worth — the fastest tongue in the West — my hands grabbin' her hot crost buns, rubbin' 'em in a pinch, and all of a suddlenly, I'm uppin' the andy, askin' her to do me more better, cut me some slacks, fish or cut bait, which is what she done, commencin' to steam up my volcano by massagin' my stallion with her undulatin' butt, 'til it rears up on its hind legs and whinnies, my Studley Do-Upright, that is, if you catch the drift o' my drafty mounted St. Ellen's.

Quick as a lightnin' rod in a thunderbolt, I yank my wallct outten my rump pocket, which ain't the easiest thing to do under these circlestances, and flash three more Georges 'n a Dishonest Abe, which should 'n does translate into "Can I finger-fuck you right here at the table as long as I do it so the bouncer don't see?" She grabs them bills so quick they mighta never been printed by the Bureau of Engravement. Before I know it, my finger finger tastes like a all-day sucker, what with that tart, tangy taste o' boys-in-berries jam.

Next, I ask her what it takes to get a "private dance" with her somewhere in the back, and she says, "That'll be two Hamiltons and a Lincoln or a Jackson and five Washingtons," which suits me just about to a T or, better, a V, if you acquire my delusion, so I dig in one more time to my rapidly repletin' wallet and grab the last o' my lunch money as she takes my hand by my fingers and leads me up some stairs behind the bar, beyond all the musics 'n lights, where I'm to get my "private *ball*room dance."

Onced in that tiny room, which is lined with shelves saggin' with toilet papers, paper towels, Kotexasses, 'n tampoons, I lose all contack with the whirl. Can you imagine no naggin' wife, no motor mounts, no excitements about the Stupor Bowl party, two days away, me 'n my three best buddies is throwin' for our old ladies, no Prez porkin' everything with two legs 'n boobs that passes his Offal Office windows 'n doors or comes in over the transit or gets delivered First-Day Overnight Prioritized Male via two-hump camel, one-horn unicorn, or Shitland pony expressed?

So, of a suddlenly, I discover myself on the floor with this gal, Julie No-Name, who, I can see now, ain't more'n eighteen nor seventeen at the least nor more, give nor take a year, with her baitin' the hook o' my pole by hand, causin' it, after less'n ten seconds, to spew a entire school o' flyin' fish.

But just about the time I get my tongue in her pussy, begin tastin' them salty sourdines, them antchovies from the Sea o' Sourdinia, that boiled bearded clam shaved smooth as a baby's pink belly for hygeniecal reasons 'n purposes, she gets mouthy 'n has to get her sixty-nine bits in by sayin' somethin' smart-ass: "Every guy in this place thinks he's a gynecologist," which commences to piss me off good, 'cause it seems feministic 'n unappreciable to accuse me o' bein' a groinocologist, 'specially since, by now, she's parted me from a grand total o' five Washingtonians, two Lincolnians, 'n two Hamiltonians, which I'm thinkin' ain't all that shabby,

considerin' all I got was about ten minutes o' her time, a little
bit o' clitoral lip-flutter on my part 'n hers, 'n a not-all-that-
swift hand job, and of a suddlenly, all that stuff I done left
behind comes floodin' back.

My tongue goes limp; my Nestie subemerges beneath the
Firth o' Froth. I begin to thaw down, lose my drive, drop my
sails for the calm I done come about in irons into. Some-
thin' about what she just done said pisses me off, and layin'
there with my pants down around my ankles and my shirt
chokin' my throat, I begin fantalsizin' my wife, big as she is,
home in bed, weavin' me into her hot charms, drawin' me into
her bodacious fat-folds, bosoms like a rhino's, hips like a
elephump's, buns so wide, belly so ripply 'n mountainous
she might as well be the Incontinental Divides, a plunderous
hipplepotamoose wallowin' in my magnificent pools o' sea-
men. I keep seein' her in all her copulence, her warm 'n ever-
lovin' glubulence, and I know I gotta get the hell outten here
'n back to my station on the motor-mount line, 'cause, for all
my negativisticism 'n maturity, I gotta emit no matter how
disgusted I sometimes get, my old lady's just a bit of A-OK
to put up with my stuff, role, so to speak, with my punches
'n pinches.

Julie No-Name, outten modesty, pulls her G-string back
into her crack, grabs up her globulous tits, 'n saunders back
out 'n down, so's by the time I get myself fully clothed
again, she's back up on stage, sittin' on the face o' the next
guy wavin' his Fathers o' the Cuntry.

Now, I'm back on 55, speedin' toward 44, sneakin' back
onto the parkin' lot without backin' off my Lake pipes, so's
not to be conspiculous, zippin' past Alferneeze, who's got
a shit-eatin' grin in his eyes, only a hour 'n a half late, him
winkin', noddin', wavin' me back into the folds (there's some-
thin' to this Confirmative Reaction stuff), and me thinkin' is
this a great cuntry or what, wishin' somewhere in the secret-
est recessions o' my wishes that our Prez hadn't made such a
publick spectrum o' hisself, coulda maybe just got some o'

them highway patrols — his private escort service — to have took him down to Q.T.'s in disguisement, maybe have escorted him nekkid — but then everyone'd reckelnize him quicker'n quick!

I guess all I can't understand is why a guy like that, even with a nut-crusher for a helpmeat, has gotta get so addictional to such young poontang. It just don't pay. Reason I like Q.T.'s so much is all you can really do is, if you're lucky 'n got a few too much stupid money to blow, so to speak, for the week, is maybe get a few minutes o' looky-feely, and if you're extra spendthrifty, get a few pussy licks 'n a hot-wax blow job at their three-minute car wash.

But that shit's all temporal 'n exotical, just a few innocent nibbles 'n grabs o' the good dough to remind a guy it's a whole lot better knowin' you ain't weavin' a trail o' lies in a spider's web that you're gonna regret whenever someone, anyone, like special persecutors 'n lawyers for the complaintiffs, start pokin' around in your private beeswax and turn up a whole herd o' tarzantulas in your basement joists, your closet lathin', 'n your attic rafters, roust out a whole flock of owls from your midnight oaks, who start in a-hootin' like they been done fowl play, when, truth be known, them's the ones who's afraid o' their own nocturnal admissions, when it all comes down to shakin' out.

So, screwin' down motor mount after motor mount with my hydraulic wrench, all I can think is I wouldn't wanna be in that dude's executal wingtips right now, what with all the whirl turnin' him into one Polack joke after another, callin' the Offal Office the Oral Office 'n such, him not knowin' who's his friend anymore, who's his enemy, for pokin' his iron in too many fires, if you acquire the drift o' my winds o' war, me thinkin' life is good, thinkin', when you get right down to Mr. Frank Nitty 'n Mrs. True Gritty, things couldn't really be too damn much better without wonderin' what planet in what galaxy you're on, thinkin' I'm excited as hell to get this Friday done so's I can go home and romance the old lady down to Stompanato's for Eyetalian, get her just drunk enough with a bottle or three o' that cheap Giganti so's we can hop in bed, rampage each other's bones, just trip the good-life fanatical and know I ain't gotta get up at four tomorrow mornin', head into Redbird's, then over to Fenton, instead lookin' forward to our Stupor Bowl tailgate key party.

I can't almost stand myself, thinkin' is this a great cuntry or what?

A Personal Story

Once, myths were essential to his well-being — gospels, fables, parables, rituals, and fictions, the noble deeds of Hellenic gods and Old Testament God, those classical and Biblical stories with their panoplies of dramatis personae, so many cautionary tales, morals to take to heart, lessons to learn to keep from repeating history or scrupulously bear it in mind . . . ah, the lowly and the grandiose, spread out across the millenniums of civilization, all of them miraculous and awe-inspiring or mired in blood and dung, describing death and regeneration or chaos and decay, everything necessary to fit the circumstances, whatever the occasion demanded, running the gamut from divine intervention, deus ex machina style, to destiny, happenstance, gratuitous fate.

These days, such theater bores him, seems almost repugnant, certainly irrelevant to his personal human drama, since he's been too busy grieving, this tormented decade, to fuss with such fustian, the smoke-and-mirrors artifice conjured by Hebrew sofers, Christian apostles, Greek poets. All those inflated stories now seem nothing more than a mountainside of flaming boulders hurled by a bellowing Cyclops at a school of migrating minnows in the ocean below, or a plague of giant locusts settling in like a heat inversion over Pharaonic fields, bringing Egypt's entire pagan population to its knees and freeing a motley of Jewish slaves at the Red Sea, only to have them reach Auschwitz alive and kicking, or a vast agony in the name of the Lord's Passion, a nailing of an emaciated, dissident carpenter to his worm-eaten crucifix so that the generations of man could inherit one more antagonistic schism to exacerbate racial hatred, to the ultimate befuddlement of cross-eyed messiahs, whose second comings presage Armageddon.

Those gospels, fables, parables, rituals, and fictions fail to distract him from his malaise; those myths can't hold a candle to his blinding pain, which began nine years ago tomorrow, Thanksgiving Day, when he watched his wife and two children drive away, abandon him standing before their empty house, never to return, standing there forever after, until he metamorphosed into a moaning stone.

Eat-Off Artist

He was so well known that when he came into the local chuck wagon, the waitresses vied, fought with each other to supply him with flesh and bones. Little did they suspect that the true object of his affection wasn't their service or fare but their *spécialité*. He craved their obsessing over him. After all, as the nation's leading authority on ribeyes, T-bones, filets, Delmonicos, and briskets, gizzards, sweetbreads, and tripe, marrow, tongues, prairie oysters, and lungs — a major-league carnivore — he had a bodacious reputation to maintain, and he truly appreciated the way they'd "meat" his needs.

It wasn't always that way, that they'd bow down and kiss his feet, show him respect accorded foreign dignitaries and USDA inspectors. Time was when he had detractors to the max, Lippmanns and Winchells and Miss Mannerses galore, who'd report his every move in public venues, analyze his anomalies, aberrations, miscues, and self-inflicted Heimlich maneuvers, his borborygmi, burps, and plangent, legume-fueled flatulence with piquant hints of onion, radish, and cabbage. To be sure, he hadn't yet mastered his forte, discovered his métier for consuming red meat off *and* on the hoof.

But he became a tyrannosaur among trenchermen, a great white shark among gefilte fish and sardines, Homo sapiens with a penchant for bleeding viands twitching or grossly undercooked, as close to raw as sushi — you might say "tartar" with a barbarian accent.

And so, his professional reputation bulged to such international celebrity that he finally bored with four-legged kine, became the Pius XII of cannibals, the Jeffrey Dahmer of the all-you-care-to-eat set, a regular at global-village eat-offs of indigenous peoples from rain forests and ice floes and deserts, subterranean caves and inner-city empowerment zones, eat-offs of whores, dwarfs, chorus lines, and kikes, eat-offs of debutantes and nubile cheerleaders, eat-offs of Black Nude Gay Miss Americas, eat-offs of missionaries from Venus and Uranus, eat-offs of Hooters skating waitresses, eat-offs of premature babies of illegal aliens, eat-offs of Elvis impersonators and O.J.'s Dream Team, eat-offs of beat-off master-race-baiters, eat-offs of U.S. Olympic lesbian delegations, eat-offs of Lois Lane, Jodie Foster, and Tom Brokaw, eat-offs of senators' wives and the lives of the saints, eat-offs that cut to the quick of the mystical heart. Oh, what delicious soupçon of the Lamb's body and blood!

Thank God he was born a Christian, not a Hindu!

Patriarch of the Breakfast Table

They've got lust in their hearts and in their sparkling, furtive eyes, the "O comarado" boys from the far side, prosaic, latter-day Walt Whitmans, lacking the old master's eye for poetic justice, seeing in a young boy's tender face sextillions of orgasms, blow jobs, ejaculations fit for a queen given to loafing all day, these fellow travelers weak sisters, albeit keepers of the faith, who've laid claim to the table beside another four-top hosting a minisymposium of twelve-steppers smug as bugs in an old hotel's moldy hall rug, each a Gregor Samsa sporting a toupee, slit of Hitlerian facial hair between upper lip and nostrils, horn-rimmed glasses à la Woody Allen, each a cigarless caricature of Groucho Marx, spouting passages from Scripture by such flawless rote (their Bibles, spread-eagled before them where plates should be, are waifs amidst extraordinary forces, useless as colonized lepers), they don't even have to open their mouths to advance to Boardwalk before passing God, collecting kudos from their cronies by way of raised-eyebrow praises to the Lord . . .

And just to their left, in animated debate, gesticulations flying like scimitars, a gaggle of Vets of Foreign and Domestic Wars, graduates of Saipan, Düsseldorf, and horny housewives next door, in holier-than-thou loaves-and-fishes robes that elevate them to the collective throne of the Johnny-on-the-Spot Café, where they spew Baptist pieties plagiarized from *The National Enquirer*, from which they net their undersea ideas, radical notions of controlling swelling populations of Lake Tanganyika hippopotamuses and egrets, clean needles freely distributed by the IRS to addicts who promise to pay their gasoline taxes, and construction of tollbooths outside the Oval Office for interns, transients, high- and holy rollers of Sun Yat-sen's Moon Dog Temple in San Francisco's Chinatown — official comings and goings — not to mention the local garden-variety venalities sprouting, blooming, wilting daily, hourly, that provide the reeking potpourri they bottle for sale at bingo nights and potlucks . . .

And, oh, the miscellaneous multitudes straggling in, struggling for a seat in this mecca, this Lourdes, Jerusalem, Benares, Lhasa — well-connected disbarred lawyers, unlicensed stockbrokers, men of the moth-eaten cloth, nuns on the rag, defrocked rabbis schlepping Israeli bonds, Kickapoo Juice vendors and Ponzi pushers, hopeful *Bedtime for Bonzo* politicos stumping for their first go as Chief Aldermanic Bottlewasher, secretaries disguised as pussies in sheep's clothing, disguised as door-to-door *Feminine Mystique* salespersons disguised as stag-party facilitators disguised as lonely divorcées, Jewish singles disguised as *Debbie Does Dallas* extras — more suck, more fuck for the buck . . .

And, of course, the one and only *me*, the Inconspicuous Grand Eavesdropper on Anonymous Souls, Exalted Mole of the Remote Nether Regions, from the Archipelago of Laputa to the treacherous shoals of Lower Upper East ben-Deezing, below the Stupendous Stoo-Roarous Chorus of Coves, where the ancient fork in the road to glory divides and those who take the Either or the Or soon discover that neither makes any difference at all.

Each ungodly a.m., this time around, I arrive, whenever the spirit moves me, at the International Date Line my shadow must cross, flying back and forth a thousand times a minute without ever so much as twitching in my seat, where I listen with deep interest, attempting to make sense of this Babelized insanity and draw conclusions to help make life if not easier for these guys — my flock, essentially — at least more salacious, obscene, concupiscent, profane.

How otherwise might I serve my congregation, keep from abetting potential defectors, apostates from my lowly chicaneries and scandals, turncoats who just might lend a cauliflower ear to that majestically arrogant douche bag of a deity, God?

Really — what's a devil to do if not nurture his krewe of dissolute poofters, fruitcakes, hermaphrodites, diesel-dykes, buggers, pederasts, transvestites, con artists, flimflam Ph.D.'s, misogynists, bigots, neo-Nazis, hijackers, misbegotten innocents and genuine victims as well, roaming gypsy bands of naive do-gooders, televangelists, charismatics, ultra-Orthodox kikes, the whole Judeo-Christian nine yards?

Jesus! I've got to make a living too, keep breakfast on the table, a cape on my back, my hooves manicured, goatee trimmed, my horns and exquisite tail sharpened.

After all, I've got a family to raise too, the family of mankind, if you will, which has grown used to a slate roof over its head in Pacific Palisades, Highland Park, Ladue, beef tenderloin and shrimp risotto on its plate.

Give me a break! Have a heart! Where would these guys be if it weren't for me? Not meaning to seem conceited or hubristic — whatever — truth is, they depend on me, and truth be told, I need them too, sort of. In all truth, it's a kind of dynamic commensalism.

So, we're in this thing together for the long haul. And attending breakfast on a hit-and-miss basis, here at the Johnny-on-the-Spot Café, when I'm in the neighborhood, is my way of fulfilling my obligation to protect and serve citizens of my bailiwick.

Never let it be said that I'm a welsher, duffer, ne'er-do-well, lazy asshole. Oh, no, not me. I keep my promises! Sho' 'nuff, boss! Never let it be said that the Big D, a.k.a. Beelz E. Bub, alias Prince of Little White Prevarications and Stretchers, don't come through when the chips is down. No, sirree! I'm here for my people, even when they can't see me eavesdroppin'.

After all, even a devil's got to keep 'em guessin', keep 'em honest.

Mr. No Longer

For reasons not easily ascertainable, he can't seem to iso-late the nature of his impasse. Therapist, family, mistress, and rabbi have compassionately counseled him, tried to under-play his increasing anxieties, attribute his growing anomie to "middle aging," quipping that it's "nothing, necessarily, more or less," "no big deal," "not to worry," "a passing phase," "just a temporary malaise," "perfectly workable, if you're willing to commit to working on it."

Yet even all their concern hasn't made it any easier for him to get out of bed or dress or shave or eat or settle on a purposeful goal to guide himself from sunrise to midnight. He can't seem to shake whatever's dogging him; it's like an October frost that won't thaw, hanging on into next August, or a brownout caused by too many people running air con-ditioners and TVs through a yearlong drought. He doesn't go to temple on *Shabbas* anymore, frequently sleeps eighteen hours on end, forgets to microwave his meals, answer his phone. His face is a thicket; his clothes are an airport urinal, and when he does go out of his apartment, he gets dizzy, collapses on the porch.

Lately, he's hatched a plan: he'd like to execute a form of self-induced euthanasia, die not by his own hand but by bribing amnesia into canceling now, then, and ever after.

Brother Onan Takes Away
the Sins of the World

He has absolutely no idea why he's awakened with the shakes today. After all, he's completely abstemious, discreet, a teetotaler in every sense of the word.

In truth, he's spent the last decade in monastic seclusion, flagellating his soul in penance, attending four masses and saying ten rosaries a day, masturbating himself bloody every few hours, around the clock, approximating stations of the cross. (His throbbing penis is the crucifix from which he hangs, tortured for his earthly sins, especially his incestuous desire to punish his father by fucking his mother, to whom he's still connected by his umbilical phallus, the Virgin Mary, the Church, his libidinous mistresses — Oedipal death wishes so overwhelming he can't discriminate between God and his dead dad, the One who made him deny his flesh and the one who whipped it with a barber's strop for confessing to "playing with himself," who beat his naked wife in plain sight of his son, yelling, "Dirty whore!" when he learned of her affair with a priest, from whom they took communion weekly.)

This morning, rising from nightmares he's repressed, he realizes nothing can save him, erase the stigmata deeply plowed in his psyche by life's torment-tractor, that monstrous machine he's driven for forty years, trying to seed and harvest his heart's fields, store up enough spirituality to last through eternity, knows he can never stop masturbating if he hopes to keep his love for the Creator alive, maintain their secret liaison unadulterated, hew strictly to his vows of poverty, chastity, hunger, and solitude. How otherwise might he lock out the world, with all its sensual distractions, refrain from repeating its human stupidities and cruelties?

This morning, he gropes for his glasses, stumbles to the

bathroom, grabs aspirin from the cabinet, throws back five with a splash of water in a desperate, frenzied effort to quell the pain, stop the shaking in its tracks.

He looks down. His penis, limp as the white rope of his black robe, is abraded, lacerated, bleeding, and scabby, a repulsive relic of his solifidian anguish. Fanatically, he strokes it until hot, screaming semen sears his eyes and ears and lips.

Stupor Bowl Tailgate Key Party

So I come sloggin' into Redbird's like Kernel Bird trudgin' acrost the south end o' the North Poles, wearin' mutt-lucks or in his bare toes — that's how woozy I still am from last night's party o' mine, my Stupor Bowl tailgate key party, that, for all I know, is still goin', though for me, it quit about a hour ago, when I fell outten bed over to Phil Brotherton's, me havin' to make it into work today, since Alferneeze turned his cheeks to my little caper Friday, when I done snuck over to Q.T.'s for lap lunch.

And wouldn't you know, with me not wantin' to hear a needle drop outten a haystack, them Cathlicks would be goin' strong, revvin' up their dragsters, burnin' excressive rubber off, smokin' up the track with their nitro fumes, run-nin' a gammon from the way the Cheeseheads done over-cocked theirselfs, endin' up in fatigual disgrace, to the Prez's dyelemma?

"Boys, anyone have his money on the Broncos?"

"Sure beat the tar out of the Packers!"

"No shit, Sid!"

"That black guy, Jorel Davis — you see the way he just walked into the end zone, strutting like the Grambling drum major?"

"He wore those big lugs down almost single-handed."

"Any of you guys know what halftime was all about?"

"Not me. I never heard of Motown, Berry Gordon either. And that music — if you can call that Africanese music *music* — was enough to make a guy appreciate the ads."

"Yeah, but what gives with an electrocuted frog?"

"And what in hell does it mean when one lizard says to another, 'We coulda been large'?"

"Huge."

"Sid, what's the difference between *huge* and *large*?"

"Don't ask me. That's just what that lizard says. I, for

one, haven't got a clue, unless it has something to do with dinosaur forefathers."

"Whatever, Sid."

"Beats me all to hell too. For my money, give me 'The Pause That Refreshes.'"

"Yeah, and I'll take a 'Good to the Last Drop.'"

"Yeah, and I'd still 'Walk a Mile for a Camel.'"

"Did any of you see the poor Pope trying to climb those fifty stairs to get into his plane? He looked like me trying to get out of the tub! And you could barely hear his voice when he'd do his Spanish prayers."

"Maybe he was disguising the fact that his Spanish sucks!"

"Who's taking bets on Clinton resigning before tomorrow night's speech? George Will says he ought to get off the pot right now."

"Yeah, and let President Gore and Tipper start to get a feel for the Oval Office and Lincoln Bedroom."

So around 'n around it goes, as always, and where it stops, nobody knows but me, which is when I finally pay my check and head over to Fenton, them guys no doubtlessly drag racin' their tongues 'til lunch, maybe all the way through to dinner, me in too much pain to be afflicted to their politikery, from throwin' such a bodacious party, excessful by everyone's weights 'n measures, since all us guys — Brotherton, Bobbit, Kowalski, 'n me, all good friends from the car plant — get together with our old ladies one night a month for our supper club and onced to year for Stupor Bowl Sunday, when, long after the game done finished, come that bebitchin' hour dictated by the bloodstreams, we call it quits, draw house keys outten a ziplick bag, and all eight of us takes off in all four directions, mixin' 'n matchin' our helpmeats (the lucky guy who gets mine not havin' to go too damn far this year, since the bedroom's just up the basement stairs from the TV/rump room we just trashed) to taste of each other's victorian spoils, if you catch my driftin' draft, none of us givin' a good shit who really wins the game (in this case, the

Elways — a shock to our systems), since us guys is always the winners, who gets to wear each other's Stupor Bowl rings, if you catch my mattressmonial drift.

I gotta emit that Phil's wife's a real fiesty piece for forty-five, if you catch the rift o' my drift. I wonder how Kowalski did with my old lady. Can't imagine him havin' no trouble navigatin' her hills 'n dales, even if she is hippopotamal — after all, she's a good sport, I guess, just like the rest o' them gals, to put up with us roughs. Then again, they could be waitin' for Welfare checks 'n such month in, month out, not knowin' what to do about gettin' sick or not. They know how lucky they got it, what with us gettin' pensions, healths assurance, perks up the ass, plus twenty-two dollars a hour to bolt motor mounts, connect stabilizer bars, install wirin' harnesses.

This here's a Merica! Life's good as it gets, even if the Prez's waved his magicianal wand, plunked his magicianal twanger, Froggy, onced too many oftens and now's gotta pay the plumber for his underarm tactics. And I guess I gotta emit that I got it pretty damn good, 'cause I ain't got his high profilement. (Granite, I don't make the big, big bucks neither nor get the credits for startin' 'n stoppin' wars in the Golf o' Desert Shield or Bozzoslobovia or get visited with heads 'n tails o' state like Meknockem' Dead, Yes-sir Afrofat, Sadman Insane, Net N. Yahoo, Nude Gangrene, 'n Dick Gladheart, here from our own fair Sho' Me State o' M.O. — and that don't mean money order!)

I mean, where else in this globular-village economy could a guy with next to little less than nothin' when it comes to any real formularized edjewcation get to sleep with his line mate's wifes without no one blinkin' a wink nor givin' a negative go-ahead nod, 'specially the guy whose wife's the object o' perfecktion, queen for a night? I mean, I ain't even too sure Jefferson Bill Clinton hisself could convince *his* First Old Lady to let him exchange keys with a Offal Office infirm who ain't even much older'n his own daughter (not that that sort o' tattoo'd ever stop me, even if I did have a underaged daughter, which the missus 'n I decided we ain't gonna never have, so long's our good luck holds out), 'specially since the Prez's old lady'd end up high 'n dry dock for the night 'less that infirm had a steady squeeze whose key he could give Hillary in a lend-lease deal. Come to wonder on it, I wonder what them two did: watch the Stupor Bowl with his cabinet, Socks 'n Buddy, maybe get a little tipsy on Friskies 'n Milk Bones?

Tell you the truth, life's great times two over three: two packs o' brewskies in three hours — frogs 'n lizards abstainin' or not — guanomole dip 'n Frito-laid chips, burnt ballpark weenies, 'n official Germanical-style potato salad. Jeezus! Where else but in a Merica can so many get so much from so few, if you catch my quotational drift? (I believe that's an approximal of a speech on ironed curtains by that English guy who was always chompin' on a fat cigar 'n bulgin' outten his penguin's suit.)

Anyways, it's gonna be amusin' to see if I get any guff from that jig Alferneeze Johnson, over to the factory, just 'cause I can't tell a Saturn engine from a hole in my ass this mornin', 'cause I ain't in no blue mood to have to defend my state o' the onion, not this mornin', not never, not in a coon's age neither, 'cause 'til I can't do my job blind, hands tied behine my hands, and still beat shit outten the Japs at their own game quality-wise, even in my wakin' sleep, drunk as three skunks copulatin' in a garbage can, I ain't gonna be imposed on, sworn at under oaths, and nobody's — no black sombitch, for damn sure — gonna excriminate me just 'cause I overcelebatcd the Stu-por Bowl too much in Phil Brotherton's bed (still don't know if Phil ended up with Bobbit's or Kowalski's) with prob'ly the best piece of ass I ever had, at least since lunchtime Friday, when Julie No-Name, with the elongated hair 'n the plum-bumptious guavas 'n the succulent snatch, done treated me like I was royalty — at least like the Presildent o' the U.S. of a Merica — for ten minutes 'n a thirty-five-dollar bill.

Is What He Isn't,
Ain't What He Was

He awakens dazed, disoriented, in a fog, you might say, a primordial fog, a miasmic mist lifting into his three brains as if from the center of the steaming Earth. He can't recall a trace of his vague nightmare; in fact, he can't remember whether his dream was a violent hallucination, firestorm raging across Mars's surface, or pastoral from the Peaceable Kingdom.

If only he'd bothered to record it, when it briefly released him at 3 a.m., he might validate his suspicion that, somehow, he's atavistic, a throwback to the Mesozoic Era, teeming with behemoths, saurian and pterodactylic creatures, amphibians redolent of colossal Gilas, chameleons.

His long- and short-term memories are defunct, if indeed they ever functioned. He can't conscion or explain his scaly skin, the spiny excrescences surmounting his tail, the raptorial claws, where just last night, he noticed his gnarled nails, remarked their need for mani- and pedicuring.

This morning, at his office, he's been testy, aggressive, muttering expletives at his fellow employees and his boss, a most peculiar behavior pattern for someone who's always been thought of not as a cold-blooded monster but as a meek, even-tempered little man with an oblique loyalty to the company that's nurtured him in its womb.

Whatever he was, whoever he might be — man or beast indistinguishable for his invisibility — he slithers from miscue to dysfunction, his ungainly snout and tail toppling chairs, tripping nervous coworkers, abrading their ankles, knees, causing some to bleed profusely, scream, crashing computers with his clawed feet, creating such chaos security has to be called in to escort him to a local hospital's psychiatric ward for extended observation, all this befalling him

in a mere three periods, six hours, destroying his modest be-
lief that his presence serves some useful purpose on Earth,
fills a necessary position in the chain of being, progresses
evolution to a degree or three or two.

Pogo Sticks

You have no idea whatsoever how you've arrived, with your private chauffeur, in your Mercedes-Benz limousine, at the far edge of a tarmac in Azerbaijan or other similar desolation you've never visited, where sits a colossal jet the length of fifty-five football fields, more like a thousand Mir space stations, if you arrange their modules to run end to end.

Nor do you have a clue as to where you acquired your Al Capone suit (bare chest showing at the satin lapels), oxblood wing-tip shoes (no socks), and worn Borsalino Panama, its brim tilted down to hide your black-and-blue shiners, absolutely no clue as to whom you might be eluding as you prepare to board your flight.

All you do know is that your instincts are telling you to assist the man with no face, no hands, legs amputated at the kneecaps, who has to bounce along on pogo sticks. You initiate assistance, gather his three attachés, and follow him up the portable stairway, into the womb of the flying machine, scheduled to depart Azerbaijan before you do.

Your assigned seat has taken a leave of absence sanctioned by state authorities to ensure sufficient room for the legless, maimed, agitated, sociopathic, who sleep in hanging baskets or cages during travel. You walk the aisle like a jilted bride, as if to an unwritten Bach fugue. You shuffle two miles down the cluttered fuselage, then exit through a door-window in the tail cone and, firmly planted on terra firma again, stare up at the fantastical jet, now revving its eight whining turbines, now taxiing up a goat path, now undulating like a hooded cobra, gathering speed, rotating, transforming the sky into a magic carpet buoying you back to the edge of a tarmac, where your chauffeur waits, in your Mercedes-Benz limousine, to pick up you and the missing pogo-stick man.

Bone Mot

Never able to disguise how excited he gets ("jumpy,"
"anxious," "high-strung," his wife would be the first and last
to assert) before taking a flight, he gets up three hours early
today, scurries from their bedroom, into the kitchen, to keep
from disturbing her sleep with his blind fidgeting, and stumbles
through his coffee-making ritual.

Conditioned as he is to doing her bidding, he anticipates
her wish that he retrieve the newspaper. Padding out onto
the front porch to assess the weather, he scampers across the
wet grass, fetches the cylindrical missive from the mailbox,
and trots back, satisfied with the execution of his own pre-
flight checklist.

Like crazed Lady Macbeth chasing shadowy hallucina-
tions through the hazy corridors of morning's castle, his
groggy wife shuffles by him in the hall without the slightest
trace of recognition. He cringes into his silence, lets her
pass, then enters on tiptoe, as if forgetting she's not still
fast asleep, and leaves the paper on the soiled sheets, where
she'll immediately see it and, he hopes, appreciate his solici-
tous deed (though he knows she won't say so).

Maybe five minutes later, maybe three, a gasping, shrill
wail pierces his ears. He winces, fumbles his coffee cup; liquid
drips down the fronts of the cabinets as he races toward the
source of the high-pitched scream and heels beside her
kneeling, naked body.

"Jesus, Nathan! See what you've done!"

"What, honey? What now?"

"Look at these prints on our new rug!"

Disbelieving, he gets down on all fours, tentatively fol-
lows their path, then sniffs suspiciously.

"Oh, Christ, hon, I've really gone and done it now, stuck
my foot in it good this time, didn't I?"

"Nathan, shut up! Run! Get the K2r! Quick! I still have to

do my makeup before the cab comes."

Spraying, feverishly rubbing with a towel an entire archipelago of tracks, he works himself into a sweat so wet it refuses to quit, keeps beading even as the taxi arrives at the airport, and all the way to Chicago.

Not until they actually get to their hotel room and he's had a chance to shower does a semblance of relaxation release him. Exiting the steamy bathroom, dripping, he hears his wife whispering into the phone and, listening, can't help cringing once again: "Yes, this is *long-distance*! Have a shampoo crew out first thing Tuesday! My dog's shit all over the brand-new carpet!"

A Surefire Shot at Heaven

Recently, having heard a provocative news report, one of those fanciful fillers radio stations mix into their programming to keep their audiences from falling asleep as they listen to details about the emerging European Community, war in Zaire, and terrorism in America, he decided to take action, do something about it, his doubt about eternity, that is, the possibility of his personally beating the odds, outliving his mortal three-or-four-score-and-ten, decided to contact the Tokyo Cyberworks, located, ironically — to him anyway — in Hiroshima, an artificial-intelligence company on the cutting edge, technology's latest Pet Rock, a company dedicated to extending life indefinitely, decided to phone for further enlightenment.

Ah, how satisfying it was, too, to actually take action, do something about something, learn that with little, if any, pain, he could subscribe to Cyberworks's growing list simply for a fee, to be determined, of course, according to add-ons of his choice (no different, really, from selecting caskets, for those still taken with the notion of earthly burial, an option rapidly dissipating in all major urban metroplexes), and receive a specially assigned cosmic e-mail address, by which he and his friends could communicate from space after his demise, indefinitely, for millenniums, eons, timespans as yet unimagined, even from within deep black holes, quarks, quasars, the company's powerful, overbyte computers able to keep the *700 Club*'s 911 permanently open, so to speak.

Ah, but he wasn't really sold on the enterprise until the pleasant voice on the toll-free line, not dissimilar to the seductive computer-chip fairy's that speaks from the recesses of his '84 Nissan 300 ZX, reminding him "Fuel is *low*," "Door is *open*," described their *pièce de résistance*, their update to the passé sperm bank of the '70s (now so obsolete as to smack of disrepute by comparison): their cryothermal DNA storage/retrieval unit, capable of retaining intact, despite all manner of attack (viruses, bombs, extraterrestrial science fiction), a few strands of his pubic hair, to be resurrected at will, his genes extracted, multitudes of himself cloned in perpetuity, on his say-so, via cosmic e-mail — surefire insurance against genealogical dead ends.

But ever a cautious, reasoning creature deep down, with a modicum of healthy skepticism under his belt as a defense mechanism against charlatans, natural disasters, and accidents of God, he finally asked the opiate voice on the other end, "What if a freak storm burns up the mainframe's surge protector, a burglar cuts the wires at Command Central, or, worse, aliens decide to nuke Hiroshima again?"

After a protracted silence, another voice, not quite identical, in fact redolent of tawdry, beguiling Tokyo Rose's, which he'd heard stroking the airwaves in the Pacific theater fifty years earlier, intruded, chanting mechanically, "Fuel is *low*. Fuel is *low*. Door is *open . . . open . . . open . . .*"

Dream State o' the Onion

"**S**ay, Traci, can you bring me some Raisin Bran?"

"Sure can, hon. Comin' right up."

"What's up, John? What's with the cereal?"

"Hey, boys. Got to get back to regular again."

"Regular? Did you ever try spinach?"

"*Spinach*, for *breakfast*? Come on, Howard."

"No, I'm serious. *Creamed* spinach is good for what ails ya."

"Hey, maybe I'll change my Raisin Bran to spinach. Traci! Got any spinach this morning?"

"You shitting me, John?"

"No, that's exactly the problem!"

Yeah, sure, I'm thinkin'. What this bozo needs is a complete ream job — on his mouth — one o' them Rotor-Rooters to come in 'n drill him a new asshole, too, while they're down there in his sewage system, 'cause he's redoubtlessly the loudest breakfast-patronage-saint Redbird's ever had in its history. Yeah, I'd like to proscribe him some Exlaxative for his brain.

Anyways, the strangest thing done happened while I was downstairs in sleep's basement last night. Musta been a bunch o' demons 'n crazies hangin' over from Stupor Bowl Sunday. Maybe I contracked 'em in Brotherton's bed, from his old lady, and it took 'til Monday night to incubait my hook. Whatever, I had the most amazin' dream last night, could hardly believe how freaked-out it was, what with me standin' up at a podial with the Presildental seals o' the U.S. of a Merica 'n the telepromoters, me gassin' all three houses o' Congress, me in the Presildent's shoes, disguised so good no one reckelnizes it's me, not the Prez, and I'm doin' just fine, readin' my unprepared speech, patched up by my spin witch doctors 'n Hillary, only Hillary's Phil Brotherton's wife, and my politicational spinners is Kowalski 'n Bobbit 'n Phil

'n, of all queer circlestances 'n random fates, Alferneeze
(I suppose to get some Confirmative Reaction, Unequal-
Opportunity-Rainbow-Coalicktion voice — no Chinks, Japs,
wetbacks, nor kikes on *my* staff, as o' this time, anyways), and
I'm readin' along all about tax repro-bates; I'm offerin' to
reduce taxes for everyone in the cuntry to a dollar a year 'n
one day's communional service workin' in a abortional clinic
to speed things along, give every livin' human in a Merica a
Master/Visa/UPS plasdick card so's they can get free medici-
nal 'n shrink benefits just by flashin' it in our new Socially
Securable System, callin' it HMO (not to be confused with
HOMO) for "Healthy Medicinal Outlook." Then I move on to
callin' all the troops home I done scattered in foreign shores
'n brothels, from Bozzoslobovia to Dad's-Bag 'n Hate-me,
since my inaugurition in 1992, callin' off all future wars per-
manaly 'n forever, vetoin' any suggestions to allow guns to
control criminals, you know, makin' a guy have to wait eight
years before bein' allowed to buy a slingshot or peashooter,
while they check out his DWI record in the Pentagonal's
superlineal mainlinin' computer.

Anyways, I'm tootin' right through this speech, and it
dawns on me I ain't gettin' no oblignatory applauds, which
I count on to let me slurp a sip o' joy juice (which is the Bud
Light I got in my handy glass), to keep my tongue nice 'n
loose, and all of a rude awakenin', it dawns on me I gotta de-
viant from my unscripted script if I'm gonna save my Pres-
ildency, since I'm in a bit of a tight, havin' got maybe the
greatest snatch o' my entire life just two nights ago over
to Phil Brotherton's house, me 'n his deluscious, feisty wife,
Marylou, goin' at it in a post–Stupor Bowl, three-hour wrapped-
up, us replayin' 'n slow-moin' all the key scores we was makin'
on each other, which was bituminous 'n debauchinal, if you
catch the rhyme-'n-rhythmic method o' my drift.

And it dawns on me that if I'm gonna save my faces with
the nation, my old lady, myselfs too, maybe (not necessarily
in this nor that primordal order), for maybe havin' had *too*

damn good a roll in the clover 'n hay with Marylou Brotherton, which could be misuninterpreted to be abmoral behavior leadin' to a infidelious addiction against the mattressmonial vows me 'n the missus done swore to in front o' man, God, 'n Minister Jim over to the Post-Tavernacle Gideon Nondenominal in Fenton, not half a block from the Saturn plant I work at . . .

That to save the eggs on my face as Presildent o' the State o' the Onion, I gotta do some real quick kiss-ass damage control — at least that's what my speechriders was urgin' me in our last meetin' in the Offal Office, two hours ago, warnin' me I better drum up a confessional or apology or somethin' to satisfy the nation that porkin' my best buddy's wife like crazy wasn't what it's bein' allegated to be by my retractors, me breakin' into one o' them Jimminy Stewart, Reginald Reagan, straight-from-the-grade-B-hard speeches, like rabbids 'n priests 'n movie stars do at the ends o' their sermons on the mount to seem persuasional and leave good tastes in everybody's mouths, so to speak, if you catch the drift o' my tongue's twist.

"Folks, truth is, all them alligators leveled against me is true."

(Applauds.)

"I must confess, I *cannot* not tell a lie."

(Applauds. Applauds.)

"I *did* chop down the cherry tree, so to speak, if you catch the wift 'n waft o' my axinal drift."

(Applauds. Applauds. Applauds resoundin' throughout the chambers in swellin' thunderclappin'.)

"I *did* pork Marylou Brotherton, but it was all consensual 'n above the boardwalks. Me 'n Bobbit 'n Kowalski 'n Brotherton's all in cahoots, and we done dreamed up the key party 'cause our old ladies seemed more 'n eager to satisfy."

(Applauds 'n screamin' 'n hootin' 'n catcalls, ceaseless 'n unendin', from the Senatobials 'n sales reps of all three houses o' commoners 'n lords, and I can tell I'm winnin' 'em over by slow degrees of increasin'ly necessarial acceptance, them members almost all men 'n almost all white, with just a few token nigs 'n Asianaddicts 'n Hispaniards thrown in for a touch o' democracy-in-progress kind o' thing, not to mention a few babes throwed in for good measurements.)

"So now you have it, folks. I done it. What's so bad? I mean, I never told Marylou to lie to her old man, 'cause he 'n me was already in the know, and we was certainly meanable. She didn't have to lie, 'cause none o' the consensual parties even give a damn. My old lady, so I been told by Mr. Kowalski (Stan the Man, to me), was one helluva piece o' work herselfs. And so it goes, tits for tater tots! I needn't spare you the seedless details, I'm sure. But there you have it, the nekkid truth. *You* be the Judge Judy 'n the jury 'n the trial. *You* decide whether I'm still fit or not to continue workin' on Alferneeze Johnson's motor-mount line at the Saturn of a Merica Automoval Plant over to Fenton, M.O. (And that don't mean money order!)

"In summational conclusions, let me just say, folks, this here's a Merica, the greatest cuntry in the globular village, and nothin' 'n no body's gonna lie to the publick. Obstructional justice is a thing o' the past. Subernational perjuritical overtures 'n under-innuendos just don't have no place in a Merican jurisprudental life. I fully intend to be your Presildent 'til my turn runs into the next guy's inaugurition, and I fully intend to hold another Stupor Bowl tailgate key party in 1999 'n 2000 'n 2001 in the Offal Office o' the White House, in the pool, in the Rose Garden, 'n in the Lincoln Log Bedroom, and I fully intend to invite my chief o' rod 'n staff, Alferneeze 'Geez, Can't See Ma Knees' Johnson, 'n my trusty kitchen cabinet: Undersexretary o' the Exterior Kowalski, Vice Sexretary o' the Uninterior Brotherton, 'n Extra Sexretary o' the Inferior Bobbit, 'n, natch, their old ladies, o' course, for sure, not to mention *my* First Old Lady, which comes 'n goes with 'n without sayin'."

(Applauds so raucous as to start the podial shakin' 'til it

threatens to topple right off the stage, exposin' me standin' there in just my executal wing tips, with absolutely no socks, slacks, no unders, no belt, no shirt from the fake turtle's neck downwards, me nekkid as a plucked peecock without no feathers . . . applauds so uproarulous I can't think o' myselfs hearin', can't hear my last salvational salvo as I rise to a pyralmid of unemotionable passions.)

"And I fully intend, next year 'n the next 'n next, to go to the post–Stupor Bowl All-Pro Roll in the Clover with whichever First Old Lady's at the end o' the key I grab from outten the hat they been throwed into (you might say I done grabbed a *new-key* outten the hat I done throwed into the ring!), and I damn well fully intend to unfulfill my campain promise to have the best damn Stupor Bowl party I can! This here's a Merica! Life's great! And it don't get no better, 'cept maybe in Sandy Eggo!"

At this point, I waken to a major hard-on, the 4 a.m. buzzer clangin' 'n clatterin', sendin' me into a urinal spasm, which, I realize, means it's Tuesday mornin', time to hit Redbird's and leave my Presildency behine.

"Say, boys, you guys owe me some congratulations."

"How come, John? Because you're a regular guy?"

"No, but I will be after the Raisin Bran."

"You too good for spinach?"

"No. Popeye ate it all last night!"

"What's the congrats in order for, then?"

"Well, it's our forty-seventh anniversary today."

"Hey, that's a real millstone, John."

"Ha-ha-ha, Sid! You've really got a way with words."

"Congrats!"

"Bravo!"

"Bon voyage!"

"Thanks, boys, but I have a confession to make. I'm still in the doghouse from Christmas. I only gave Gladys one gift because she kept saying, 'Let's not give all those gifts this year,' so I took her at her word, and when it came time to opening the gifts, she was real hurt."

"Was the one gift any good?"

"Sure! Of course! What do you expect? But today I have *eleven* gifts. Got them all at Sam's Club."

"Sam's Club? Jesus, John!"

"Hey, wait, boys! I got her half the store, even a real good gold cross in the jewelry department."

"Oh yeah? *Real* gold?"

"Hey, it wasn't cheap!"

Me thinkin', as I pay Gert my overdue check and head for the plant, shame the way some guys short-shift their old ladies, take 'em for granite. Jeezus! Can you imagine bein' married to the same broad forty-seven years and then, on top o' that, buyin' a bunch o' shit, a carload, to try 'n cover up the quality deficit, and then, on top o' that, expectin' your old lady to wanna compile with your wishes to manhandle her, after plyin' her with analversary bubbly up the ass, when all you do is give her a gold-plated cross? Women get a raw deal, I gotta confess — if only in my dreams!

There Was an Old Man

He had so many children, the old man who lived in a shoe, he didn't know how to pull himself up by his boot-straps. (Naturally, black-patent-leather Johnston & Murphy wing tips don't easily do double duty as pointy-tipped Frye shitkickers.)

And that, in a pistachio, was the conflict. He couldn't explain how it came to be that he was riding Dolly Madison, that profoundly vicious prize Brahma bull in today's rodeo. After all, he felt rather foolish flopping up and down, sideways, stark naked (apparently, on filling out his entry card, he confused "side saddle" with "bareback"), in front of a packed crowd of Puerto Rican inmates, on permanent loan from Rikers Island, and CEO's from Microsoft, Anheuser-Busch, and Frito-Lay, especially in his three-hundred-dollar Johnston & Murphys, which he usually kept shoetreed, in their felt dust covers, in the recesses of his shoe house, res-urrected once, maybe twice, every five years (his shoes, not his shoe house) to guide him in the path of righteousness, let him form the tenth spoke in a *minyan*-wheel, do his part in bearing a pall from the synagogue into the earth, the closest these Johnston & Murphys ever got, before now, to sullying themselves with loose clods of funereal dirt.

But try as he might, he couldn't fasten to his dress shoes the brass-and-steel spurs they gave him as souvenirs for en-tering the rodeo, as if this ferociously bucking Brahma bull needed the additional taunting of his heels digging into its scarred flanks, each time leaping for the moon, hanging sus-pended in midair, each sweep and thrust of its vast torso threatening to throw the old man, flailing in his simulated wing-tip boots, onto the ground like a bee swatted out of the sky by a maddened cartoon bear, casting him, finally, in one insanely corrupt eruption, to his contused and bloody back, in plain sight of the rioting convicts, doing life for

serial murder, first-degree sodomy, bestial genocidal acts pat-
terned after those of your garden-variety *Einsatzgruppen*,
and leaving him there for dead, like zebra meat clawed into
unidentifiable pieces of a jigsaw puzzle, the old man lying
there helpless, numb, dazed, drooling, his naked body parch-
ing under a blistering sun, his double vision locating him at
the center of a great field teeming with daisies or black-eyed
Susans, mile upon efflorescent mile, an entire Third World
nation of refugee children, his children, all those who lived
in the shoe he didn't know how to pull up for its missing
bootstraps, that shoe neither boot nor metaphor (though
he could never have made this link, since what he was best
suited for doing was trying to keep order among his family
members, the multitudes who shared his shoe size, the con-
tours of his cosmic domesticity), rather synecdoche (he
wouldn't relate to this either) for the shabby human con-
dition he laced up around his spirit each day on waking,
as though it were the thin waxed strings of his Johnston &
Murphys, in which he conducted all his business, as if they
(the shoes, not the laces) might lend to it (his business, not
the human condition) a sense of dignity, instead of the nylon
cords of the straitjacket into which, one day in his sleep, they
fitted him, exchanging one hallucination for another, a newer
variation on not knowing how to pull himself up by his
bootstraps.

Stabbed in the Back

He wakes up with a backache so excruciating that raising himself from his bed, from the dead, becomes Ptolemaic, a matter of formulating equations to construct a Rube Goldberg series of pulleys. He might as well be a two-ton block of chiseled rock to be dragged, Nile-barged, dragged again on sledges by ten thousand straining slaves before being hoisted into place on the pyramid of Zoser-Cheops-Chephren-Mycerinus — his monument to eternal sleep — instead of a guy who can't move despite trying for half an hour. No innovative manipulations with arms and hands or contortions with legs and torso succeed in elevating him to his elbows.

By now, he should be showered, dressed, out of his small apartment, floundering in traffic, dreading the next eight hours in the pits, but stasis is a mummy case. He's a spent scarab on its back, unable to rectify or deconstruct his helplessness, project his feeble voice enough to penetrate the thinly insulated walls separating his rented chamber from the myriad labyrinthine shoeboxes surrounding him like vaults, catacombs, and corridors buried deep in the Valley of the Kings; nor can he reach the phone, under a pillow on the floor, plead for assistance from 911.

He can't remember such a painful dilemma, threat to his self-sufficiency, his immediate health, welfare, his actual survival. Suddenly, he realizes he could easily lie here until he dies, rots in silence, turns to dust, surfaces from this hallucination, brought on yesterday afternoon by his permanent termination from Cairo Quarry & Mines.

Preowned-Vehicle
Account Executive, Late Again

Damnation! Tarnation! Holy incarnation! How could this have happened to *me*? It's the worst catastrophe in years, decades, maybe a century or millennium. Who knows for sure? It just might be the worst recorded disaster in the history of mankind, the world, the universe.

What the hell could I have possibly done to bring on such a debacle, calamity, fuckup of enormous proportions? I deny all complicity in this bungled mission, this human-computer hard-drive crash. I swear it wasn't pilot error. Oh, no! The devil's in the details again!

It could've been the CIA or FBI on a botched search-and-seizure operation, mistaking me for a Colombian drug lord or some kind of New York cocaine pusher, or it might've been agents from NASA, breaking into my bachelor's launch pad, hoping to find stolen moonrocks.

Honest to Pete Rose, the apostle Paul, and Queen Mother Mary of Scots, by God, I swear on a stack of Gideons, King Jameses, a thousand and one Douays, and the Old Testament as officially authenticated, sanctioned, blessed, and designated one-hundred-proof parve, that I had nothing to do with this screwup.

As to how I'm going to concoct a valid excuse for coming in an hour and a half late to Big Bob's Chevy + Geo City, I can't say. The boss will never believe aliens from space landed on my bedstead while I was sleeping, mistook my alarm clock for some secret Star Wars weapon, but they did, and in their haste to escape with their prize, they broke into its internal works, changed my wake-up setting out of ignorance, and dropped it before fleeing empty-tentacled.

Fuck! This is the third invasion in a month! One more, and my pay gets docked, and I get put on probation.

Lottie Savage, Colored

When she finally passed (she lived, they conjectured, to a hundred and one or four), three undertakers fought over her body, got in an ugly bidding war as to which mortuary would earn the bragging rights to gussy up ol' Lottie Savage to the nines, deck her out in Miriam Haskell cultured pearls, her earlobes and neck glistening with costume jewelry, a rhinestone giraffe pinned to the lapel of her triple-marked-up hand-me-down outfit, dredged out of Galadney's Thrift Shop basement next door (none of the visitants any the wiser that her double-knit jacket and leather skirt unevenly cut off at the kneecaps — some teenager's skirt in another incarnation — were thirty-five years soiled, if a day), send her off all refined-like in a tiptop-of-the-line, state-of-the-art, mirror-lined, Circassian-walnut casket, with nothing but the best of sprays — orchids, stars-of-Bethlehem, birds-of-paradise (no mere roses or spider mums for Lottie Savage), no matter that on the way from Bosley's Funeral Parlor to St. Mary's of All Martyrs and Saints (no matter that she was a nonpracticing Baptist of the Southern fundamentalist per-suasion), and again from the Catholic church to the Free-at-Last Burial Refuge of St. Louis (wedged between the munici-pal airport's two main runways), the converted-Winnebago hearse overheated, twice needed roadside emergency assis-tance from Troupe's Towing Company (the first call turned out to be a close call rather than an embarrassment — the part-time driver actually had antifreeze, succeeded in getting the vehicle restarted — not like the second rescue, when the Holmes tow truck ended up leading the procession, past taxi-ing jets, to the freshly dug grave under a tent fit for a crowd of a thousand, sheltering three miscellaneous waifs and a somewhat tipsy freelance preacher).

But apparently that was just the beginning, not the end, of Lottie Savage's demise and burial. Her surviving relatives back in Okolona, Mississippi, insisted she be disinterred, her mirror-lined casket transported by private rail car to the land of her people, her ancestors (as close to the shores of Gambia as practicable, anyway), for a down-home, down-right down-to-earth tribute, a fitting service to be witnessed by an indigenous God, not a mealy, big-city Northern God without fire-and-brimstone vengeance aplenty for sinners.

And they got Lottie's bones, her sepulchered body, but not her earthly estate (an estimated $75,000 from the sale of her shack at fair-market value, once it was eminent-domained because it just happened to be blocking the path of a half-built shopping center in need of unanticipated expansion for a flaw in the initial planning of the job by its original, subsequently-fled-to-Chile developers), which, doubtless, motivated their familial piety, since, once the many hands that clawed into her pie got their fingers sticky with its sweet filling, all that was left were a few crumbs to be swept off the table, onto the floor, and hauled away in the morning trash — Lottie Savage's last effects.

In the Brain-Terrain
of the Walking Dead

What happens when you send all your energy on a spe-
lunking expedition into the brain's cave or a climb into the
imagination's rarefied air, where breathing is accelerated to
such a degree even forgetfulness is screened in Technicolor
and the blood makes love to its DNA in public?

You awaken from dreams, sweaty and fatigued to the
bone, dreams that might be white-lightning clouds, icebergs
of dead-pygmy heads floating in a cauldron-sea, beached
whales bloating with bleached maggots until, so swollen,
they explode, one each minute for hours, seconds, however
long it takes to splatter sleep with offal, cause all harpoon-
ers adrift in their dories to call off the hunt, return to the
Pequod resigned to chasing clouds, icebergs, and whales
on a night when the moon is at full height, capable of il-
luminating the brain-cave and fancy's blizzard-enshrouded
mountain, to whose base or peak you'll descend or ascend
when you marshal your energy, regain your strength from
last evening's trek to land's end, where you went, always
go, by yourself to hide from dream-demons, mind-parasites,
recover from another day of defending yourself against
the bends, altitude asphyxia, crises you experience just try-
ing to exist in your eight-to-six job, dispensing numbers
to callers demanding information published in white- and
yellow-page directories, seekers phoning in, lazy and impa-
tient, with whom you'd like to protract your brief conver-
sations, asking them whether they ever see whales scaling
the summits of McKinley, Everest, the moon, breaching the
Ligurian and Dead Seas, beaching on shores haloing Laputa
and the islets of Langerhans, flooding caves catacombing
man's deepest secrets.

If only you could ask them, extract answers as to what

happens — what *really* happens — when they send all their energy out on expeditions to the center of the earth, the farthest stars in the galaxy, and it never returns to awaken them, awaken you, from the sleep of the ages.

Karla Mae

To save my ass, I can't fathomize how them mackerel snappers, supposin'ly law-abitin', God-fearin', consensual adults, can carry on so about the new Lezzie Borden, Karla Mae Fucker, the pickax killer o' Texass 'n all parts west.

But that's the topical o' their gabfest this humpin'-day Wednesday mornin', when, onced more time, all I'm tryin' to do is get a vice grip on one more day at a time, preppin' myself for the assemblage line over to Fenton, but not bein' able to for all their clatter 'n humpdrum monotonizin', havin' to listen to them amater legal theologinians measurin' out the merits 'n dismerits o' givin' that reborn-again bitch a second chance, who done stabbed two victims, fifteen years back, square on in the chests 'n heads 'n groins, with mallets 'n after-forethoughts, premedicative, that hatchet lady, Karla Mae, tryin' to make the Mother Superior Court o' the land 'n the ex-Presildent Gubernor Bushed real suckers, her tryin' to get 'em to buy into her findin' God, repentin' her sins, gettin' a inside track on the Bible, unrecriminatin' herself, and me wonderin' if what them loudmouth hipplecrits is sayin' is they should let that bitch crawl off her meat hook, get away from that legal injection Scotch-free, get to eat off us taxpayers for the rest o' her normal, abmoral, reborn-again lifes, and her with a husband behine glass, the one who reconverted her to Jesus' tenderized mercy 'n such, who she can't even touch nor have conjubull sex with 'cause that ain't in the Lonely Star State's constitutional.

Who knows? They let her live off the fat o' the land, compute her sentence from dead meat to life on skid's row, she just might come down pregnable by immaculate perception. (Them things always seem to happen in *The Natural Enquirer*.)

So they're carryin' on about how she done found God, which she emitted to all the TV shows — *Charles Grossman, Perry Ballwell, Okra, Davis Letterer, Cheetah Riviera, Wheel o' Misfortune*, 'n, for all I know, C-Spin. Truth is, she got a helluva lot of attentions for her imported turnaround in findin' religion.

So these guys is debatin' the measures 'n weights o' crapitalized punishments, sayin' how they heard Texass ain't douche-bagged a gal o' the femalian kind since the Civil War Among the States and that she's gonna be the first to get the ax — if you catch the draft o' my woody's ax shaft — ever in the mammary o' Dallasonians 'n Houstonites. I can hear 'em goin' at it like it's a Presildental rebate, talkin' up mercy 'n dissolution o' sins, one of 'em comparin' commutin' to communion, gettin' the two real mixed up, from what I know, 'cause the snappers can commit sins up the ying 'n yank and get off every time (knowin' it in advanced) just by repeatin' a few mesmerized hose-annies to Mary's mother and stringin' a few dozen cramberries on strings for the church to put on their Xmas trees at Xmas, along with popcorn, pretzel, 'n potato-chip strings 'n Jap-made lights 'n such. . . .

But a few of 'em's arguin' like pitted bulls that if they let her off the meat hook, she's gonna open up the corral's floodgates for every pitted bull in any Chink shop in any Chinktown in Chinkland to ax shit outten his or her boss or wife or line mate or mayor or even Sadman Insane just 'cause he or she don't like the color o' his or her eyes or the way she or him won't let he or her get in hers or his pants after him or she done wined 'n dined her or he to beat all shit — you know, anyone'll be able to light into anybody, enemy or foe alike, and be able to claim he or her done found God, got the endlightenment 'n the revolution and don't intend to commit insalts 'n batteries again, promise never again to stick a shiv in his or her husband's or wife's gut 'n into her or his boyfriend's or girlfriend's neck, like O.J. Stimpson done or any o' them other cereal-murder rapists runnin' hellbent for selection all over loose 'n gone.

I mean, Jeezus, if these guys is so used to gettin' off just by sayin' a few roseberries 'n eatin' 'nilla wafers, then you can almost understand how they'd take up with this broad's side. As for me, myselfs, 'n I, it's a eye for a I, a pickax in the tits 'n dick for its coeffishin's, plain 'n simplistic! I say give the bitch what she deserves and say good riddlance to bad rubbish, say goodbye to yesterday's fish, if you catch the draft o' my driftin' whift!

Jeezus! What this cuntry don't need is a bunch o' religional fantastics 'n left-wing evandalists invitin' every diesel-dyke Lezzie Borden with axcess to a midnight-special ax to go around flauntin' her genders and thinkin' just 'cause she's got a sensationable set o' jugs 'n a open-for-beeswax drive-thru-fast-food taco fritoholy stand sittin' right there out in plain sights of all them Mother Superior Court justices 'n the ex-Presildent Gubernor o' the Alamo that she can commit embezzlements o' grave bodily harm and inspect to get away with it 'cause she's the weaker o' the three sexes 'n deservin' special pity.

Fack is, they want to give her a second chance, then maybe she 'n me can exchange places. I'd like to be served three squares with a roof over 'em and let *her* bolt down motor mounts five days a week and see how long *she* lasts from the stresses 'n metal fatiguals to the brain 'n such, just see how long 'fore she walks back onto death's row, where, with a little luck (granite, hers done finally run out), she can posepone gettin' her dose o' legal joy juice for another decade or change of admenstruation, when someone might just decide that anyone claimin' to find God under her mattress, inside the barbells, under the license-plate-stampin' machine can walk Scotch-free outten the front door and start from scraps into bein' a downrighteous 'n unuptstandin' citizen who promises not never to ax no one again for life.

Jeezus! Where *are* we these days? Emitted, a Merica may be the globular-village stuporpower, but just bein' that don't give us the rights — does it? — to take away the sins o' the whirl like them mackerel snappers is tryin' to say Jesus done.

Come on! How'd them guys like it if they done dis-covered their priest was a ax-rapist who emitted he done cleavaged his mistress's old man 'n kids but said he should still get off Scotch-free 'cause Jesus turns both cheeks for assholes who bare a cross? I bet to hell they'd be the first on the picket-ax line to have his nuts castorated, and I damn well guarangoddamnteeya that even Pope John Paula Jones III hisself wouldn't petition ex-Presildent Gubernor Bushed to send Archduke Regalia back to his death's-row condo in Fulsome Prism for a life o' floggin' his Friday-night flounder 'n grindin' his own Saturday-night-special ax in the "manual arts" shop, if you catch the happy-hands-at-home drift o' my hands-on shaft's draft.

Settling for Unleavened Bread
on the Road Out of Egypt

He could tell it was going to be a rough Sunday morning (seven lean seasons after seven plenteous) when the server behind the counter (obviously a trainee in training for the duration of eternity) handed him a murdered bagel so blackened on the edges — black to the core, carbonized beyond a diamond's hardness — he'd need saber-toothed-tiger teeth, the frenzied jaws of a piranha at feeding time, or a McCulloch chain saw to render it chewable.

But when, ten minutes later, he had to reject his second burnt offering as defective goods, toxic, hazardous to the health of even streptococci, and suggested the flunky reprise the maneuver, turn down the heat on his Topf and Sons toaster, at first all he got was an autistic stare.

"You asked for a dry bagel, didn't you?" the nonplussed lackey queried.

Feeling profoundly victimized, Mr. Put-Upon paused before retorting, trying to hold back a snide barb.

"Yes, but *dry* doesn't imply a cow carcass in a desert just outside Santa Fe or a firestorm on Mars."

He might have erupted into sardonic laughter, tickled by his own mordant humor, had his eyes not focused on all four bagel halves, still perched atop the counter like roasted chickens from the kitchens of Auschwitz. As it was, all he could muster was disgust, impatience with the fellow's stupidity.

Somewhat indignant himself, the kid lashed out, "You said dry! And these're dry!"

"Dry means *plain*, unbuttered! Just toasted! Dry!"

"Hey, bud," the server abruptly fulminated, "you can go fuck yourself! I'm tryin' to please everybody's needs in this dump, but I'm just one guy, not a mind reader! To me, dry means well-done, seared, scorched; to the next guy, it's butter or margarine on the side."

"Why don't you just shove the Fleischmann's up your rosy-red rectum, *bud?*"

By this time, they had an audience poised to applaud their vaudeville routine. But just then, the manager materialized from the back and broke up the contretemps with a stroke of genius.

"Order anything you want. Breakfast's on us. How about strudel, stollen, schnecken?"

"How about my dry bagel smothered in cream cheese and lox?"

"How 'bout cremated cheese and rocks?" the trainee carped.

"On second thought, skip the bagel. I'll have matzo to go."

Dennis the Doorman

No wife, no kids to go home to — no home, either, for that matter, just a fleabag, rattrap one-room dump in a rent-by-the-day/week tenement teeming with seedy transients, on the western edge of the city's ghettos, where urban blight rubs shoulders with decrepit white flight, does a danse macabre, night and day, in plain sight of the sleazy, seething humanity who populate this Ho Chi Minh Trail.

In truth, he considers himself fortunate to receive the pittance of alimony that arrives the first of each month, punctually, at his P.O. box. Without his ex-wife's modest subvention of his government disability pension for wounds to his spine and cranium incurred in Laos, Cambodia, or Vietnam (he doesn't remember, maybe never even knew, for the grass haze cocooning him in those days), his job wouldn't make ends meet.

His entire past is encapsulated in a single frame: that afternoon he came back to St. Louis, toting a musty duffel bag, wearing an attitude of come-what-may, standing at his front door, ringing the bell, Sandy peering through the curtain in disbelief, answering barefoot, naked, too stunned to refuse him entry on her lover, he too confused to recognize a gook about to heave another grenade his way, or to take cover before the shrapnel flew.

And that was all there was, the present collapsing into the past like a black hole, a coal shaft imploding, his life cut loose once again, as it had been in Southeast Asia, one vast numbness, a cataclysm of land mines, napalm, rifle fire, rain, snipers hiding in rice paddies . . . his doorman's day shift a place to go where he knows every face and no one will throw a grenade.

The Toad

> . . . *him there they found*
> *Squat like a Toad, close at the ear of* Eve;
> *Assaying by his Devilish art to reach*
> *The Organs of her Fancy,* . . .
> — John Milton, *Paradise Lost*

I have a major advantage over most people: whenever I want to hide from the world, or myself, all I need to do is find the most raucous café in town, light at a table or booth *in medias res*, and take up specs, pen, and notebook. The rest is duck soup, a piece of cake, what, in the trade, we call easy as pie, a walk on the wild side without ever stepping outside for a bite of reality; it's a ballpark wiener smothered in mustard and relish.

No one can hide better than I: suppression, repression, forgetting — I can cry Alzheimer's like nobody's business, like others cry wolf, at the drop of a sombrero, stovepipe, straw-boater. I wear a million different hats, depending on the slant of the sun's rays at midnight — the chapeau artist of the Show Me State, a real go-getter when it comes to disappearing, throwing up a screen of smoke and mirrors, shimmering illusions, simulacra.

Oh, don't ever doubt a pro, pal! With my tricky Bic-wand, I can manipulate a Pharaoh out of his visions, interpret his dreams like no Joseph who ever lived, wind a boa constrictor around any Houdini who brags he's not chained to his dissimulations. I can rewrite history with a flick of the wrist, twist kaleidoscopes to set rabbits and doves free. Ah, and I can make a Holocaust exterminate Hitlerian ambitions without risk of being Hanseled and Greteled to a crisp, just by ridding my pen's tip of death wishes.

You'd never believe the lucubrations, the Seuss-like tongue-stumblers, Twain-stretchers, bombastic, six-page Faulknerian convolutions I've committed as Chief Wordsmith-Magician to the Prince of Lies. You'd be surprised, by God, if you could see the ease and expertise I display, hiding from the naked truth: that, as Plagiary and Paraphrase Wizard of the Nether Regions, I've never owned an original image or idea, have been living on borrowed time, so to speak, to write, hiding from the demons inside my slimy hide.

Mr. Late-Nite TV

He does few maneuvers well, especially for a human being, but he excels at eating and sleeping. In fact, he's perfected these routines to such a complete degree, he's recently been invited to host his own TV show, which has him in a bit of a dither only because he's never really stopped long enough to figure out how he's carved such a big niche in a worldwide market, turned these commonplace arts into sciences.

For three weeks on end, he's watched Oprah and Rosie and Geraldo, Ted Koppel, Tom Brokaw, and Charlie Rose; he's viewed reruns of Paul Prudhomme, Graham Kerr (the Galloping Gourmet), and Justin Wilson (the "I garontee" Cajun cook); he's even perfected the selling techniques used on the Home Shopping Network and practiced them in his vanity mirror; he's learned to clap at the drop of Vanna's hat, as they do on *Wheel of Fortune*.

And now he feels as though his hour is nigh, that he's ready to make the leap, take the big multimedia-syndication step into the world of the rich and famous, where he'll cast a lasting shadow, leave a radical legacy for future programming that will be emulated for years to come, a landmark show like *Dragnet*, *All in the Family*, *M*A*S*H*. He even has the format and image in place: his character will be a composite of Archie Bunker, Ralph Kramden, and Fred G. Sanford.

He'll spend the entire hour on stage in his pajamas. His props will be a table and a bed, obliquely lit in stark green neon to render a semblance of the sleazy Floridita Hotel on Easy Street in Tijuana's red-light district, a bizarre effect calculated to attract the curious as well as youthful devotees of *Beavis and Butt-Head*. A Busby Berkeley staff of thousands in black tie will arrive with steaming tureens, spread his table with a moveable feast, facilitate his trencherman's orgy, until, about halfway through his nightly feeding frenzy,

he'll begin to yawn uncontrollably, grow noticeably somno-
lent, lethargic, comatose, need his entourage to transport
him from table to pallet, kick-start him to recite his prayers
while they lullaby him with Negro spirituals, send him off
to the happy hunting ground counting fleecy sheep and
beefy bison as his audience swoons in a serenity transcend-
ing death, achieving a silence so satisfying, salvific, they fall
asleep with the TV snoring to beat all hell.

Biographical Note

L.D. Brodsky was born in St. Louis, Missouri, in 1941, where he attended St. Louis Country Day School. After earning a B.A., magna cum laude, at Yale University in 1963, he received an M.A. in English from Washington University in 1967 and an M.A. in Creative Writing from San Francisco State University the following year.

From 1968 to 1987, while continuing to write poetry, he assisted in managing a 350-person men's clothing factory in Farmington, Missouri, and started one of the Midwest's first factory-outlet apparel chains. From 1980 to 1991, he taught English and creative writing at Mineral Area Junior College, in Flat River, Missouri. Since 1987, he has lived in St. Louis and devoted himself full-time to composing poems. He has a daughter and a son.

Brodsky is the author of thirty-seven volumes of poetry (five of which have been published in French by Éditions Gallimard), nine books of scholarship on William Faulkner, and three books of short fictions. His poems and essays have appeared in *Harper's*, *The Faulkner Review*, *Southern Review*, *Texas Quarterly*, *National Forum*, *American Scholar*, *Studies in Bibliography*, *Kansas Quarterly*, Ball State University's *Forum*, *Cimarron Review*, and *Literary Review*, as well as in *Ariel*, *Acumen*, *Orbis*, *New Welsh Review*, *Dalhousie Review*, and other journals. His work has also been printed in five editions of the *Anthology of Magazine Verse and Yearbook of American Poetry*.

ALSO AVAILABLE FROM *TIME BEING BOOKS*

EDWARD BOCCIA
No Matter How Good the Light Is: Poems by a Painter

LOUIS DANIEL BRODSKY
You Can't Go Back, Exactly
The Thorough Earth
Four and Twenty Blackbirds Soaring
Mississippi Vistas: Volume One of *A Mississippi Trilogy*
Falling from Heaven: Holocaust Poems of a Jew and a Gentile *(Brodsky and Heyen)*
Forever, for Now: Poems for a Later Love
Mistress Mississippi: Volume Three of *A Mississippi Trilogy*
A Gleam in the Eye: Poems for a First Baby
Gestapo Crows: Holocaust Poems
The Capital Café: Poems of Redneck, U.S.A.
Disappearing in Mississippi Latitudes: Volume Two of *A Mississippi Trilogy*
Paper-Whites for Lady Jane: Poems of a Midlife Love Affair
The Complete Poems of Louis Daniel Brodsky: Volume One, 1963–1967
Three Early Books of Poems by Louis Daniel Brodsky, 1967–1969: *The Easy
    Philosopher, "A Hard Coming of It" and Other Poems*, and *The Foul Rag-
    and-Bone Shop*
The Eleventh Lost Tribe: Poems of the Holocaust
Toward the Torah, Soaring: Poems of the Renascence of Faith
Yellow Bricks *(short fictions)*
Catchin' the Drift o' the Draft *(short fictions)*

HARRY JAMES CARGAS (editor)
Telling the Tale: A Tribute to Elie Wiesel on the Occasion of His 65th Birthday
    — Essays, Reflections, and Poems

JUDITH CHALMER
Out of History's Junk Jar: Poems of a Mixed Inheritance

GERALD EARLY
How the War in the Streets Is Won: Poems on the Quest of Love and Faith

ALBERT GOLDBARTH
A Lineage of Ragpickers, Songpluckers, Elegiasts & Jewelers: Selected Poems
    of Jewish Family Life, 1973–1995

ROBERT HAMBLIN
From the Ground Up: Poems of One Southerner's Passage to Adulthood

WILLIAM HEYEN
Erika: Poems of the Holocaust
Falling from Heaven: Holocaust Poems of a Jew and a Gentile *(Brodsky and Heyen)*
Pterodactyl Rose: Poems of Ecology
Ribbons: The Gulf War — A Poem
The Host: Selected Poems, 1965–1990

TED HIRSCHFIELD
German Requiem: Poems of the War and the Atonement of a Third Reich Child

VIRGINIA V. JAMES HLAVSA
Waking October Leaves: Reanimations by a Small-Town Girl

RODGER KAMENETZ
The Missing Jew: New and Selected Poems
Stuck: Poems Midlife

NORBERT KRAPF
Somewhere in Southern Indiana: Poems of Midwestern Origins
Blue-Eyed Grass: Poems of Germany

ADRIAN C. LOUIS
Blood Thirsty Savages

LEO LUKE MARCELLO
Nothing Grows in One Place Forever: Poems of a Sicilian American

GARDNER McFALL
The Pilot's Daughter

JOSEPH MEREDITH
Hunter's Moon: Poems from Boyhood to Manhood

BEN MILDER
The Good Book Says . . . : Light Verse to Illuminate the Old Testament
The Good Book Also Says . . . : Numerous Humorous Poems Inspired by
    the New Testament

JOSEPH STANTON
Imaginary Museum: Poems on Art

FOR OUR FREE CATALOG OR TO ORDER
(800) 331-6605 · FAX: (888) 301-9121 · http://www.timebeing.com